STAGE CITY

Tracey Rebel and his cowpunchers knew it would be tough blazing a cattle trail from Texas to the Arkansas Valley. They were right. It was wilderness for most of the way, peopled largely by bands of Apache, Comanche and Ute. But when the herd finally reached the Santa Fe Trail, trouble hit the Texans hard in the shape of the notorious Charlie Dodge and his band of desperadoes. Even then, things would not have been so bad but for the lovely unpredictable Esther Masterton, sole survivor of the wagon train which Dodge and his outlaws had ambushed.

STAGE CITY

STAGE CITY

by

Jefferson Fraser

Dales Large Print Books
Long Preston, North Yorkshire,
BD23 4ND, England.

British Library Cataloguing in Publication Data.

Fraser, Jefferson
    Stage City.

A catalogue record of this book is
available from the British Library

ISBN   978-1-84262-880-5 pbk

First published in Great Britain in 1957 by John Long Limited

Copyright © John Long Ltd., 1957

Cover illustration © Michael Thomas

The moral right of the author has been asserted

Published in Large Print 2012 by arrangement with
Jefferson Fraser, care of Watson, Little Ltd.

Dales Large Print is an imprint of Library Magna Books Ltd.

Printed and bound in Great Britain by
T.J. (International) Ltd., Cornwall, PL28 8RW

CONTENTS

1

DESPERATE MEN

At four o'clock in the afternoon the man dismounted at a water-hole. He knelt low, scooped water with his hands, letting it run over his lips and beard. Beside him, reins trailing, the mustang's dust-caked muzzle slobbered in the life-sustaining liquid. Dodge got up from his crouched position, hauled cruelly on the reins, forcing the animal back, pulling hard so that the steel bit sawed at the pony's soft mouth. Dodge stood breathing hard, head thrust forward and evil gaze steady on the trembling beast, daring it to move.

The mustang's thirst was still unsatisfied, but fear of its master was like an iron curb, stronger even than the instinctive desire and need to drink.

Dodge took the canteen from the saddle, knelt and filled it, drinking now from the metal neck and then let the water spill down him, saturating his shirt, cooling his skin. When the mustang edged forward with nostrils flared, he called: *'Hold it, I say!'* and refilled the canteen, stoppering it carefully, his sloe eyes on the horse.

'Go git it!' This time there may have been a softer quality in the rasping voice. If that were so, it was only by way of contrast with the harsh venom in that first utterance. The pony swung its head, rolling its eyes, making first sure that the man's hands were empty save for the canteen. Then it reached forward and dipped its nose into the water, drinking a little, raising its head and drinking again as it had been schooled.

Dodge moved out from the blighted cottonwood's shade and scaled a wall of rock on his left. His searching glance laid itself along the trail; on into the shimmering distance.

The oven temperature of full summer beat down on this shadeless stretch of the Santa Fé Trail, burning into rock and shale until the land itself threw out an acquired heat of its own, drawing every drop of moisture out of the breeze that drifted lazily from a distant line of cottonwoods and willows.

Yet, now that Dodge had slaked his thirst, he squatted atop the rocks, seemingly impervious to the crowding heat; intent now on the far-distant dust cloud. It was scarcely a cloud at that, and few white men would have seen anything at all to denote the presence of travellers. He drew papers and sack from a shirt pocket and lowered his eyes only the once, tipping dry, black tobacco dust into the cornpaper before dexterously rolling and lighting the quirly in a near-continuous action.

After about a half-hour he could see the lead-wagon, faint as yet in the sunlit dust haze, and presently he had made out six or seven big Conestogas. So much the better they were not Murphy wagons driven by a bunch of tough bull-whackers and mule-skinners! That would have meant a hard, bitter fight, likely with many of his men killed or wounded.

He estimated that the lumbering train was now about five-six miles away. Less than two hours from now, those Santa Fé bound traders would be pulling off the trail, preparing to camp after another long day's grinding trek, and Charlie Dodge allowed himself a tight, ruthless smile and made his plans and waited there with all the patience of his Arapaho forbears.

He could afford to feel some satisfaction, even though the real work lay ahead. For it was no accident, this; no blind chance which had drawn him here, but the result of much riding and a deal of watching. Scarcely had he been out of the saddle these last eighteen hours, so thorough were his methods, thorough as an Indian's or a catamount's and every bit as cruel.

When he realized the *cigarrillo* was finished he built another, lean sun-blackened fingers making no more a task of it than might be performed in pulling a blade of bunchgrass. He climbed down from the flat-surfaced rock, more aware of the sun's strength as he exerted himself; feeling the heat of his underwear and wool shirt and trousers stretching tight against his flexing muscles. He stepped from the sandstone and stood watching the mustang as it tugged at grass and shrubs no more than a dozen yards yonder. It half-raised its head and turned a wary eye on the man's hands; satisfied, it returned to its foraging.

Dodge hunkered down under the cottonwood, figuring this thing out and hazarding a guess at the value of each wagon-load. It was the same train, of that he was sure. Yesterday at dawn he had counted eight Conestogas thirty miles from here. Today he had made the tally six or seven. But there could be another wagon still out of sight.

Well now, this had come at the right time. Idle men were dangerous men, and doubly so when the cash ran low and tempers, already short, were pulled tight as wet buckskin drying in the sun. Mostly, Dodge thought, the wagon-trains were dying away, slowly, yet inevitably, as coach and rail transport began to take over. For more than five years, nearer ten maybe, there had been rich pickings along the Santa Fé Trail. This was still lawless country for the most part, and Charlie Dodge's hard-case gang had rarely been troubled by the inadequate and hastily-mustered posses. No, it was not the law which threatened their existence, it was simply progress. Other methods might have to be tried, other Territories visited where the birds could be plucked. Meanwhile, the first likely train in several weeks was on its way and there was work to be done.

He stood up now and his actions were at once decisive and smooth. He tightened the cinches and gathered the trailing reins, lifting up into the saddle with all the lithe ease of a savage. For a while he held the mustang to a quick run, and shortly settled into the more prudent routine of travel: a walk, a quick gallop, and walk again.

By these means Dodge brushed the lower foothills of the Mesquite, aiming for the shallow basin which, through careful judgment and reckoning, he was reasonably sure would be the wagon-train's camping place tonight.

Above, in a darkening sky, lay the glittering wash of stars. To his right the low Mesquite hills stood faintly visible, their scrub-dotted crests blackly etched against an indigo back-cloth.

No sounds disturbed the quiet of early evening except the mustang's hoof-beats, muted by grass; the jingle of bit and chain, the soft squeak of saddle and stirrup leather. The breeze freshened and became a wind, travelling from the westward river to chill this summer-hot land throughout the hours of night.

Dodge keened this wind as he rode, absorbing the aroma of sage and sun-cured grass and the faintly definable scent of water; vague impressions which came to a man's nostrils only to be cast aside with selective instinct. For there was no menace or danger in the infinite variety of Nature's subtle scents. Only in the reek of fires, of cooking, of gunsmoke and horses and men there sometimes hung real threat to a man's survival.

But now he could see the winking lights of scattered fires, before which dark shapes moved with flat-footed weariness. A quick, sudden veering of the wind carried camp sounds to the ears of horse and rider. The mustang's ears flicked forward and back and Dodge made no move to muffle the warning nicker. He took care to 'halloo' the camp in good time, coming up slowly, and drooping in the saddle, declaring himself in every silent but informative gesture as a tired traveller far from the trail to home.

A big, blocky shape loomed up from the semi-darkness ringing the nearest fire. Several men paused in their preparations for supper and sent their direct and questioning glances at the jaded rider. A woman looked up, natural bashfulness forgotten a moment through the very strength of an inherent curiosity.

'Howdy, stranger.' It was the big, bearded man whose rumbling voice rolled through and over the lesser sounds of the camp.

In the firelight the dust-caked face of Charlie Dodge assumed an expression of mild relief. Slow-smiling, slow-talking, he offered the minimum explanation which was due from any stranger seeking another's hospitality.

'Bin ridin' some, these last three-four days,' he drawled. 'Headin' fer a new settlement called Piñon Creek. Guess I musta taken the wrong trails a coupla times or more. Name's Charlie Clagg, mister…'

'I'm Joseph Wishart.' The big man half-circled the bright-burning fire, held up a paw and shook the rider's hand. 'Light down, Mister Clagg, an' welcome to what we got to eat an' drink, which mebbe ain't much…'

'I'll be grateful just the same.' Dodge smiled and stepped from leather and moved well into the fire's light, understanding quickly that an attitude of simple straight-forwardness would go down best.

Wishart's head bobbed up and down approvingly. He turned to the stooping woman and modestly her eyes lowered to the smooth, flat stone on which she had been rolling and cutting dozens of flapjacks.

'Sary! We gotta guest for supper. Come

15

over here, woman.'

She arose and quickly wiped her floured hands on a gingham apron. She kept her glance now on Wishart's face, except for one swift look into the stranger's hat-shadowed eyes.

'This is Mister Clagg, Sary, headin' for a place called Piñon Creek, I guess. But right now – here!' Wishart broke off and filled a tin cup from the huge coffee pot suspended across one end of the fire. He thrust the vessel into Dodge's hand, grinning amiably. 'Drink that, Mister Clagg! Mrs Wishart's cawfee can put new life into a man. Say! Likely it'll be a half-hour yet before suppers' ready, but if you'd sooner we pack yore saddle-bags with grub...'

'No!' Dodge burnt his tongue on the hot java and remembered to curse in silence. 'I ain't in all that hurry, Wishart. 'Sides which, apart from bein' really hungry, I – I guess I'm feelin' pretty tuckered out...'

Mrs Wishart's thought transferred itself to Joseph's mind through the medium of her lightning glance.

'Reckon you can bed down under our wagon for the night, if–'

'Look, Wishart.' Dodge's voice slipped dangerously close to its normal tone and he smiled at once, flashing white teeth to smooth away all churlish roughness. 'There ain't no need to go to any trouble, Wishart.

Me, I'm usta ridin' long hours. Just a meal an' a rest, some feed for the hoss mebbe, an' I'll be off.' He blew on the coffee, sipping now with noisy relish. 'Mebbe,' he grinned, 'I'll decide for once not to ride out first thing. Likely I'll still be asleep under a bush when yore wagons pull out at dawn...'

'If you'll excuse me.' Sarah bobbed her head towards the cooking and waited for her husband's nod before returning to her task. Perhaps, Wishart reflected, he could understand something of a lone wolf's desire to be free and unfettered; to ride or rest as the mood took him, indebted as little as could be to the rest of his kind. He drew a short-stemmed pipe from his shapeless coat and struck a match to the partially charred dottle.

'Sure, Clagg.' He puffed blue-grey mushrooms of smoke, regarding the dark, hatchet-faced rider over the sulphur flame. 'I understand.' He jerked his head in the direction of the arced wagons, vaguely silhouetted beyond the glow of fires. 'Most allus I aim to have them wagons movin',' soon after six o'clock. Seven at latest. That means everyone risin' around four-thirty, foraging for brush an' deadwood, cookin' breakfast...'

Dodge drank the remnants of his coffee and spat out a tongueful of grounds, wiping the long drooping moustache with rope-

17

burned fingers. 'Yeah! Reckon you folks has a pretty long day, anyways. Two-three miles an hour mebbe for ten hours a day. Reckon though you'll find it's bin worth it, when you hit Santa Fé. I guess that is where you're headed?'

The wagon-train captain nodded, a simple eagerness momentarily lightening his face. 'You bin to Santa Fé, Mr Clagg? You know what things are like there – if – gen'ral merchandise an' manufactured goods still fetch good prices? Oh, sure. We all heard from other traders that things is fair to middlin'. But 'ceptin' for our guide, none of us's bin there as yet...'

'Your guide?' Dodge asked quickly. 'What's his name? Mebbe I – well, even if I did get lost a coupla times, takin' cut-offs, I bin along the Santa Fé Road before. Met a few guides from time to time, so I wondered...'

'Sam Lawler. Likely you'll see him afore you leave. Knows his job when it comes to pilotin' a wagon-train.'

'You have any trouble?'

Wishart slowly shook his head. 'Not real trouble, I guess. Not like some o' them earlier freights trains usta meet up with – Injuns, outlaw gangs and the like. No. 'Part from one man drowned when we was crossin' near to the big bend of the Arkansaw, nothin' but a few minor casualties.' Wishart stared around

18

over the firelit camp for a moment before finishing. 'Mebbe we bin real lucky at that. Them Pawnees, f'r instance, they was watchin' us for several days...' The captain's chuckle held its quota of reminiscent satisfaction. Then: 'You was tellin', Clagg, 'bout Santa Fé...'

'Yeah. But you got me kinda fogged, mister, on that Pawnee story, on account I heard the Injuns was often partial to a small train. 'Specially like when it was plumb occupied crossin' a river!'

'True, friend, but like I said, we was lucky. A coupla times when things looked a mite scary, we sighted cavalry an' I guess them Injuns saw 'em too. After that, 'bout a week later, I reckon, we came on a party o' Kiowa – leastways, that's how Mr Lawler had 'em figgered...' Again Wishart's belly-rumbling chuckle. 'Sam told us to put on a big show with all our guns, y'know, doin' a mite of fancy shootin' and letting them redmen see how good we was...'

'Shouldn't 've figgered you had an army of sharp-shooters here.' Dodge's sloe eyes had been busy all the while, and under the pretence of a sober interest he had listened with part of his mind only to Wishart's story. The rest of his cold, ruthless being had centred itself upon the acquisition of as much knowledge as he could gain through swift yet cautious glances at the surrounding

19

scene. Impalpably, his face sharpened with interest as he glimpsed the stacked interior of Wishart's wagon just as Sarah reached over the tailboard for utensils.

'No more we ain't got above sixteen rifles,' the captain acknowledged, 'and only Sam an' mebbe six-seven of the men can shoot real good. But them Kiowas saw enough, way Mr Lawler an' Henry Bootes fixed things…'

Dodge became acutely aware that his own turn had come. Wishart expected an answer to his question and it should not be difficult to keep these folk entertained during supper, regaling them with word pictures of the ancient Spanish town towards which the freighters and traders still headed. Ever since 1822, when William Becknell's wagons had swathed a trail through the waving buffalo grass, this westward hejira was repeated annually from springtime to early fall.

The dark-featured man grinned as others from the nearer wagons gathered round their leader's cooking fire.

'I'll tell you what I know, Wishart,' he said affably.

It was a grimly satisfied Dodge who rode from camp and pointed his mount towards the sheltering Mesquite hills. Yes, there had been some risk in posing as a lone and trail-weary rider. For there was always the chance of coming face to face with someone he had met before. Lucky that Wishart had volunteered certain information at the outset, including the name of their guide. And whilst Dodge knew, by repute at least, such men as Carson, Jed Smith, Dick Wootton and Tom Tobin, the name of Sam Lawler had rung no warning bell.

As things had transpired, and despite Wishart's simple confidence in the guide, Lawler had proved to be no more than an ageing frontiersman, taciturn and indrawn, evincing no more than a brusque interest in the captain's guest. How could Sam Lawler, veteran of a half-dozen campaigns from Leavenworth to Taos, know that this man called Clagg in reality bore the dreaded name of Charlie Dodge? The same merciless half-breed who, with his forty-odd band, had scourged the Santa Fé Trail with deeds of dark violence!

Even at night Dodge had no trouble finding his way along cut-offs and through brush-choked gullies which might well have appeared impassable to most riders. Thus it was still early night when he put the mustang to the last narrow rock fissure and reined in, calling out the pass-word in a low, carrying voice.

'Okay, Charlie.'

Starlight glinted on a rifle barrel and a man's shape loomed for a moment out of the night and, as always, Dodge's recognition was immediate and certain.

'What news, Perch?'

'Everything's quiet an' peaceful right now,' Perch Lindrith answered. 'But yesterday, Foley got drunk an' threw a gun on Sid—'

'*What?*'

'Sure, Charlie. But by a lucky chance, Sid was holdin' a tin cup in front of him. The slug—'

'You mean Sid's all right?' Dodge's voice was hard and thin, and deadly like a war arrow, tipped with poison.

'Sure is.' Lindrith stepped closer, holding his voice low to match the leader's. 'The cup saved him, I reckon. Two-three of the boys jumped Foley then an' took his gun—'

'He bin kept tied up all the while?'

'Sid saw to that.'

'Go fetch Sid now, Perch. Tell him I want to see him *presto* and to bring Foley along too!'

'Sure, Charlie. You figger to wait right here?'

Dodge nodded. 'Make it fast, Perch.'

The guard slipped into the shadows, reappeared in a moment leading his pony. He slid the carbine home under his right leg and hit leather, rowelling his mount across the rough, rock-girt ground to where a wide, shallow basin opened out in the velvet darkness beyond.

Dodge waited with an evil impatience, his

22

mouth drawn tight as the jaws of a closed steel trap. He picked out the glow of several screened fires ahead and for a rare, intuitive moment the desperado wondered how much longer he would be able to continue using this natural hideout. Perhaps it was the Arapaho blood flowing in his veins that at times like this prompted such strange, mystic feelings of unease. In part, at least, the mood could be due to more material things, like the gradual decline of freighted goods along the Trail; the increase of military traffic; the still ineffective yet growing threat of law establishment in places which only a year back were as wild and primitive as any along the whole frontier...

Riders shaped out of the night and hooves drummed on the buffalo grass and shortly clattered over the stony stretch. He saw that Foley was well flanked by Lindrith and Sid, the unfortunate man's hands roped behind his back.

'Howdy, Charlie. Perch said this was how you wanted it!'

'Yeah.' Dodge turned his gaze on Foley, letting it bore into the heavy-bearded face. 'You started a gun ruckus, Foley, on account you'd bin hittin' the bottle. Way I heard it, you drew on Sid an' dam' nearly robbed me of a good lieutenant! Well now, what you got to say?'

'Ain't much sense denying it!' Foley's voice

was deep and flat, utterly lacking in expression or cadence. 'Too many hombres around for me to claim otherwise.'

'I reckon you know what's goin' to happen now?'

In the starlit night, Foley spat tobacco juice from his iron-hard mouth before turning to the horseman on his right. 'You make it good an' quick, Sid, clean through the heart, an' I'll be waiting' for you right by the gates with a mug o' cawfee.'

'How 'bout it, Charlie?'

'You fix it, Sid, an' not too close here. There's some nosy folks allus figger they got to find out what them big turkey birds is after.'

'I know the place. Two-three miles is all. Should not take much more than an hour.'

Dodge said, 'Get back as soon as you like. We got a job on tomorrow which will mean ridin' before dawn.'

Sid nodded, reining his mouth over towards the rock entrance. A nine-foot rope had been tied to the bridle of Foley's horse, the other end was lashed to Sid's saddle. The two riders moved out, and presently, with a brief nod to Lindrith, the gang leader gigged the mustang forward into camp.

Men lay or squatted in closely packed groups, amidst an incredible array of riding gear and various piles of equipment. Saddles, ropes, carbines, blankets and a thousand-

and-one odds and ends lay scattered around in the light from the screened fires.

Dodge looked at Sid out of button-bright eyes, and most, if not all, the watching men saw and understood that significant interchange of glances. Nothing like a sharp yet silent warning, the 'Breed reflected, to remind these hard-eyed criminals that their leader's rules could not be disregarded under any conditions whatsoever. He sat on a tree-stump, head and shoulders thrust forward and elbows resting easily on his knees.

'There's seven-eight wagons camped off the Trail,' he informed the silent throng. 'And no more'n sixteen rifles all told. Only a half-dozen men at that, as can really use 'em.' He waited for the deep throated growl of pleasure to subside before continuing.

'They're Santa Fé bound, an' reckon to break camp right early in the morning–'

'When do we start ridin', Charlie?' Blaze Curragh asked with a twist of his thin lips.

Dodge, in high good spirits now, laughed softly, setting the signal for an easing of the tension with which the very atmosphere had been charged since Foley's forced exit.

'They ain't so far away, we got to ride out *pronto*,' the outlaw leader told his men. 'Takin' the short cuts I reckon we've got mebbe five-six miles. But by the time we've half-circled them, comin' in from the north an' east, then likely it'll be nearer nine or ten.'

'Now. The way I got it figgered, the best time to jump them is around six o'clock. Mostly they'll still be finishin' camp chores, out in the open and away from the wagons…' Dodge smiled in sly anticipation. 'The captain's a big, bearded hombre over six feet an' I got a feelin' he's mebbe useful with firearms. We see to it, then that he's one of the first, an' along with him we fix the guide, a gent by the name o' Sam Lawler–'

'Lawler?' It was Hank Knell who spoke. 'I guess he'd be the feller I met up with once or twice back in Kansas. Was an Injun scout an' far as I recollect worked with the army one time.' Knell paused and shook his head thoughtfully. 'Must be gettin' old in the tooth by now. Kinda past his prime, I'd say.'

'Yeah! An' I figgered likewise, Hank, when I saw him 'bout four hours back.'

'You shore haven't bin wastin' any time, Charlie.' Sid grinned. 'Seems like you got this job purty well lined up.'

Like most of his kind, the gang-leader could lap up considerable quantities of syrup and not sicken of it. 'The exact spot,' he told his appreciative audience, 'is about a coupla miles eastwards along the Trail from the cottonwood water-hole. Over to the far side there's buffler grass an' shallow canyons–'

'Guess that'd be just about whar we

26

hijacked them two Concords back in early summer.'

'You got it, Mel!' Dodge pushed back his black, dust-powdered hat. 'Cawfee, Sid,' and waited while his lieutenant filled a cup from the big iron pot over the fire. He poured some of the burning liquid down his throat and once again ranged the close arc of men with his glittering gaze.

'This place, you remember, is mebbe a good camping ground for wagons...' He leaned forward, the feral expression on his face intensified by the play of flickering firelight and shadow. '...But it's also the right spot for an ambush and I'm bettin' that whatever's in them Conestogas 'll be worth a little trouble!

'What we do is this,' Dodge continued. 'Get the men first off, 'specially this feller Wishart, the captain, an' Lawler. The rest'll be easy. Sid here will fix for some of you to strip one – mebbe two – wagons of all the domestic junk an' such-like, then load up all the stuff they'll hold. Once we got them away an' stashed close to here, we'll be all set to drive 'em to the Fonda–'

'One thing, Charlie. If we're fixin' not to burn them other wagons on account of the smoke showin' clear, then ain't there a chance that any survivors – some o' the wimmen, mebbe–?'

'We cain't afford to leave any survivors,'

27

Dodge rasped. 'We made that mistake with them Murphies last year an' it took nigh on three weeks to shake the posses off'n our tails.'

'Sure,' Sid agreed. ''Tis the safest way, Charlie.'

2

RED MORNING

Tracey Rebel lifted a hand in signal to the rider watching a quarter-mile distant and then turned his pony away from the bedded down herd towards the silent camp sprawled in sleep beneath the paling stars.

Shortly he stepped down from the saddle, moved across to one of the blanketed shapes. 'Wake up, Pinto. It's four o'clock.'

Like an animal, the oldster was awake almost before Rebel's words were ended. He sat up, yawned and stretched and gazed up at the clear, lightening sky before reaching for trousers and boots. He watched Rebel step amongst the circle of prostrate forms to waken Garston, the other dawn guard, and Chuck Barringer, the Long Rail cook. Whilst the three men roused themselves for the chores of another day, Tracey dropped fresh brush onto the fire's dying embers and in a little while flames began to reach out and hungrily devour the tinder-dry kindling. At the right moment, the Long Rail foreman began feeding driftwood from the nearby stack. Lastly he filled a kettle from one of the chuck wagon's water barrels, toted it back, and poured the water into a huge iron coffee pot suspended on a tripod over the fire.

Pinto, bow-legging his way back from the remuda, pulled on his saddler's reins and stared as Tracey searched around for four tin cups.

'Ain't you hittin' the hay? You got a coupla hours' sleep due to you!'

Garston, a sober-faced man, joined them. 'That's right, we done well enough so far, Tracey. You don't haveta ride yoreself spurs an' all!'

Rebel grinned, accepted the quirly which Pinto handed him and stuck it to his mouth. 'Well,' he conceded, 'we sure've trailed close to fifteen hundred head of fat steers, better'n six hundred miles.'

'They ain't so fat now, Tracey.' Garston lifted the coffee-pot lid and furthered his calculated pessimism by adding, 'An' we still got a tidy way to go, ain't we?' He filled one of the cups, drinking down the lukewarm coffee and wiping bearded lips with a shirt-sleeved wrist. 'Guess I'd better git over an' relieve Rede.' He started to head for the cavvy and paused long enough to throw his final comment at Tracey Rebel's feet. 'Like I bin sayin' all along. What makes you figger anyone's gonna buy them long-horned, four-legged savages?'

The Long Rail foreman smiled easily, despite his realization that a deal of truth lay in the others' words. Nor was Zing Garston the only one of the crew with some doubts at least. Even Pinto and Rede were a mite sceptical; had been ever since John Bartlett returned from Colorado with the crazy notion of *driving* cattle to faraway markets which he claimed existed. But all this didn't mean the Long Rail crew were not fully prepared to trail clear across the Canadian border – if Bartlett or Rebel figured it necessary.

'Mebbe some o' these miners an' railroad men are getting sick of buffalo, Zing, an'...'

Garston gestured non-committally and continued on his way.

'Herd'll be milling around soon,' Pinto grunted and poured hot java into two cups, handing one to Rebel. Chuck Barringer was already busy at the wagon's tailboard, cutting strips of pork and mixing flour and water flapjacks in preparation for breakfast.

'I'll ride over with you, Pinto,' Rebel said, scattering the grounds from his cup.

'Hell! Ain't you seen enough o' them brush-poppers these last weeks 'thout settin' there gazin' at 'em when you don't haveta?'

Tracey nodded absently and stepped into leather, his mind probing ahead, worrying a little, despite the fact that, so far, they had come through with an astonishing minimum of trouble. A few times recently, parties of Mescalero had shown their resentment, as far as several swift interchanges of shots. Yet mostly they had seemed more disconcerted than hostile; perhaps confounded somewhat not only by the sight of an army of long-horned shaggy creatures, herded by these dark-skinned riders, but also by the incredibly rapid fire emanating from the white men's hand guns and rifles. An improved model of the first five- and six-chambered Colts had appeared, and Texas was Sam Colt's stamping ground anyway. Likely enough the Apaches had not yet seen these six-load guns in action before, nor the latest Henri and Spencer breach-loading rifles.

Out of the early mists swirling from Ute Creek, Rede jogged into clear view, stopping to exchange a brief word with Garston before aiming for camp and maybe snatching an hour's sleep before breakfast.

At a walking gait, Pinto half-circled the stirring herd, running an experienced eye over the undulating sea of shaggy backs and long-horned heads. At last he neck-reined the cow-pony and headed back to where Tracey still gazed northward, as though he would see what lay ahead along the miles still to be covered. But Tracey Rebel could not know that before long his whole being would be centred somewhere up there. Nor yet could any dreams or visions of his reveal that this same route would later be followed by Charles Goodnight and Oliver Loving, trailing their herds ever onwards, clear through to Cheyenne. New trails were indeed waiting to be blazed by men who had the vision and the strength.

Pinto reined in. 'Didn't you say yesterday we was gittin' purty dam' close to the Santa Fé Trail?'

'Sure, mebbe no more'n a few miles ahaid. Why, Pinto, what's on yore mind?'

The puncher shrugged, yet for all his studiedly casual air, his glance touched Rebel's shadowy face with a half-wistful expression. 'Jest figgerin' I'd like to have seen that town, Tracey. They say when a wagon-train gits in, the place goes crazy wild. Plen'y liquor an' food, black-eyed *señoritas*–'

Rebel's smile cut through the oldster's words. He twisted in the saddle, nodding towards the awakening camp. 'You know what they're like, Pinto. Ready to fight – kill if necessary – 'specially when it comes to defending anything wearing a Long Rail iron. But give 'em some back pay and a night in town, well…' He grinned. 'I guess it wouldn't work out, doin' a thing like that in the middle of a drive. Mebbe we can take in a few places on the way back. In any case, the boys'll be paid off in Stage City – provided the buyer J.B fixed with don't duck out of the deal.

'Camp's wakenin' up now,' he added. 'Let's take a *pasear* yonder.' He pointed ahead towards a series of low, scrub-dotted hills, and with the wild exuberance of their kind, both men spurred their mounts forward, while the eastern sky brightened and flared, slowly at first before exploding into a thousand kaleidoscopic patterns of gold and madder-pink merging into cerulean and pearl-grey and the palest shades of saffron and violet gentian.

Breathless and windswept, the Long Rail men drew rein atop the first grassy crest, and their gazes, swift-moving and steady, spread out to cover this newest vista on their journey north.

'Once we've got the herd over these hump-backs, Pinto, and across the Santa Fé Road, we'll be all set to drive clear through to the Arkansaw Valley–'

From way ahead, the distant sound of gunfire carried on the breeze; not isolated shots, but volley after volley with scarce a pause in between.

'Injuns, you figger, Tracey?'

Rebel's face had tightened, his whole attitude alert, watchful as though he were poised ready to spring.

'Whatever it is,' Pinto muttered, 'will surely be through long before–'

'Two-three miles yonder, at most, an' plenty of trouble by the sound of it! We–'

'But—'

'Listen, *amigo*. Get back *pronto* and bring Rede, Steinhaus and Jimmy. Leave Zing in charge an' tell him to hold everything till we get back.'

'What—?'

'Fan the breeze, Pinto!'

Rebel's glance slewed round to cover the hard-faced men on either side of him as the bunch drew rein in a juniper grove.

'The Trail must be just below those bluffs ahead. Stick here while I take a look-see.'

'How long since you an' Pinto heard them first shots, Tracey?' Rede Blakmer questioned. 'Sounds mighty quiet right now!'

Rebel nodded. 'Forty minutes, I guess, near enough. Even if the fight's over, likely there's someone needin' help.' He swung down from the saddle and moved out towards the line of low sandstone escarpments. Cautiously he edged his way forward, half-prepared for anything or nothing, and then shocked at the scene laid out before him less than a half-mile down the Trail. For a long moment his gaze crawled from one end of the devastated camp to the other, seeing enough even at this distance to understand something of the fiendish thoroughness with which the attack must have been planned and executed. Wagons had been turned over and wrecked, obviously pillaged of everything that the robbers deemed of value.

Rebel could see no sign of life or movement down there, and slowly he climbed to his feet, dragging his gaze away as Pinto hurried forward, in his hands a pair of service-worn glasses.

'Okay. So you said to stay put, but I figgered I saw somethin' movin' over to them foothills—' He broke off abruptly, narrowed eyes taking in the full impact of the slaughter below. 'That don't look like Injun-work, Tracey, else them wagons would 'a' bin fired, I reckon.'

Grim-faced, the Long Rail foreman took the proffered glasses, turning them toward the distant smudge which Pinto had indicated to the south-west. Boulder and brush and scrub-growth bulked into his vision as he quickly focussed on to a large party of riders, leisuring their way toward the brush- and aspen-dotted foothills.

'Close to thirty riders,' Tracey gritted, 'an' travelling so slow an' peaceful, a man might figure— 'ceptin they're all pretty well armed an' meaner lookin' than sidewinders.'

He swept the cavalcade again, more slowly this time, and suddenly held quite still, not moving nor yet describing what he saw. Pinto edged closer to his side.

'What's up, Tracey? You figger this the bunch, even though they's ridin' like they was goin' to a picnic?'

Rebel lowered the glasses and handed them back. 'They got one of the wagons over to one side – didn't spot it first go. But worse than that, Pinto, they got a girl...'

The oldster's blue eyes took a moment to accustom themselves to the lenses. The sun was above the eastern hills now, its oblique rays dazzlingly bright and touching distant objects with a mirage-like aura of light. Yet almost at once Pinto found and held the scene and quietly cursed.

Rebel turned, signalled to the men waiting by the junipers and held them with his remote gaze as they trotted their mounts over, Toke Steinhaus leading the foreman's saddler.

'Bigawd!' Pinto muttered. 'Yo're right, Tracey. They got a woman an' it shore looks like she's tied to that saddle. Say! I reckon they stopped – holdin' a pow-wow...'

Rede Blackmer swung his bearded face towards Tracey, his pale yellow eyes hard as amber stone because of what he had just seen down there across that trampled buffalo grass.

'You fixin' to do something, Tracey boy; we ain't got all day. What's the set-up exactly?'

'You've seen what's down there, men. No one left alive, I'd say. But right now we haven't got the time for a closer look. This wagon-train was being attacked when me an' Pinto heard them shots earlier, an' the killers are not so far away, nor in any hurry it seems. They've kidnapped a woman...' Rebel's glance moved over the three mounted men... 'You can figure what that's goin' to mean! There's around thirty desperadoes in this band.'

'How we gonna copper their bets, Tracey?' Jimmy Yoakum drawled.

For a brief moment the Long Rail foreman regarded this nineteen-year-old boy whom he had dragged from a Ragtown deadfall two years back.

'Figger you could find a trail an' pin those buckos down from this side, Jimmy, until Rede an' Toke can open up on their other flank?'

Yoakum slid from leather and stepped across to where Pinto still watched and took the glasses from him. Shortly, he turned to Tracey and nodded. 'Looks like I could reach 'em all right in around twen'y-thirty minutes, without advertising the fact. How long's it gonna take them two mossyhorns yonder to join in?'

'Watch yore lip, kiddo,' Blackmer growled. 'Me an' Toke's got a sight more ridin' to do and there ain't so much cover.'

''Stá bueno,' Jimmy grinned and stepped into the saddle, swinging his head round to Tracey Rebel. 'Sure hope this carbeen don't get all heated up like the old one did. I got thirty shells in all, boss; what's the play?'

'Make good an' sure to leave the back door open before you start pumpin' lead. Then scatter them, 'specially the two ridin' herd on the woman. Soon as you drop them, Jimmy, Pinto an' me'll ride in and snatch her – if we're lucky! Meanwhile, Toke an' Rede'll be covering us. Soon's yore ammunition is gone, get to hell out of it an' meet back here.' Rebel's grey-eyed glance touched them fleetingly. 'If the thing misfires, then each man'll haveta high tail it back to camp on his lonesome, as best he can! All right, Jimmy. Fan the breeze!'

Yoakum touched spurs to his paint, pointing it to a shallow gully scooped out of the escarpment. He had made his choice of route quickly and well, for they could see now how a natural trail sloped and twisted its way through sandstone and thickets of greasewood and mesquite. Tracey turned to Blackmer and Steinhaus. 'You all set?'

They nodded and Rede said, 'We cut across the Trail right here an' burn leather all the way. Mebbe they'll spot us soon enough, but I reckon they ain't likely to start anythin' till we's real close.' He jerked his head at Steinhaus and gigged his mount forward over the bluffs. Together the two riders descended the shallow gradient, and shortly hit the grass-verged road at a dead run. In a moment they were thundering across at a tangent to the devasted camp.

Rebel gathered the trailing rein and stepped into leather and Pinto flashed a last glance along the Trail before following the ramrod's lead.

'They's round a bend right now, Tracey; mebbe a little more'n three miles yonder. We got a fair chance of catchin' the bustards flat-footed, I reckon.'

'Sure. Surprise! That's our Ace-in-the-hole, and I'm bettin' the last thing these hard-case hombres would expect is a handful of riders loco enough to attack 'em!'

'Yeah. Now you come to mention it, I guess we are purty crazy at that. Seems like I remember we's supposed to be hazin' a herd o' steers for a feller called John Bartlett. Now where I heard that name before?'

'Reckon he must be the guy who pays us,' Rebel answered, narrowed eyes momentarily catching sight of the distant moving speck which was Jimmy Yoakum. 'Still an' all, Pinto, I cain't see any Texan jest standin' by while a woman's carried off...' He paused, gaze traversing across to where Blackmer and Steinhaus were racing their mounts towards the as yet unsuspecting band of outlaws.

Unlikely that many more minutes would elapse before they were either seen or heard, cutting across the frequent open stretches of country north of the Trail. Nor would it be long before Yoakum started in with his carbeen.

'Let's go,' Tracey said grimly, 'an' show them coyotes a thing or two!'

Once clear of the bluffs, the Long Rail pair touched spurs to their eager mounts, and hooves pounded the short tawny grass at an ever-increasing tempo. At this lower level it was no longer possible for either of them to catch any glimpse of Jimmy, and only once, just for a flashing moment, did Rebel sight Rede and Toke as they burst from a thicket maybe two miles distant, sweeping towards their quarry beyond the Trail's bend with all the skill and savage purpose of Comanche horsemen...

For the first half-hour since quitting the scene of their evil work, Dodge and his men had kept a sharp look-out, especially on their flanks and ahead to where the narrow trails and cut-offs quartered towards the Mesquite foothills. Despite such routine precautions, a mood of arrogance and self-satisfaction quickly settled over the band. The supreme contempt in which this wild bunch held all things lawful and sacred showed itself increasingly as watchfulness and tension slackened. It was there in the very way men sat their saddles with slack indifference; it showed again in their coarse speech and crude jokes, repeated as often as not for the express purpose of bringing a surge of flame to the pallid cheeks of the girl whose life Dodge had spared for one reason alone. With a few, like Blaze Curragh and Whitey and the man called Mel, the game held a deeper satisfaction. For this golden-haired fury, young as she was and so recently compelled to witness the brutal massacre of her friends and relatives, had turned at one moment from a terrified girl to a wild animal brought suddenly to bay. Like a female catamount she had sought to savage her attackers, nails clawing, teeth snapping, until the cursing Mel had knocked her down, gazing at her lissom form with a mixture of mad anger and desire.

She had sunk sharp teeth into the middle finger of Mel's left hand, biting to the bone. She had furrowed Curragh's stubbled cheek from eye to jaw with her bloody talons. Now, as the desperadoes held their mounts to the wagon's lumbering gait, Blaze Curragh no longer scanned the country behind. Instead he let his imagination centre on the slim figure lashed to the saddle of Hank Knell's horse.

He spared little thought for Knell or Jo Buckskin. Neither man would have further need of earthly possessions, and so the only point of interest lay in speculating as to who would win their saddles and horses and gear in the draw which Sid invariably organized under these conditions. But right now, Curragh was more concerned as to how he could persuade Mel or Whitey to change places with him. The girl rode between her two guards, helplessly tied; even Knell's sorrel was held on a long rein secured to the bridle of Whitey's dun. But where was the sense, Blaze wondered, in even thinking about her? Very soon the whole cavalcade would be threading its way through the brush and scrub oak and juniper covering the approaches of their hideout. Once there, Charlie would take the girl and keep her in his shack. Only if a man were strong enough to brace him, and possessed the requisite nerve and ability to out-gun the 'Breed— Curragh stopped there, feeling the sweat seep from under the brim of his hat and suddenly appalled by the idea. Yet, paradoxically, it held a crazy kind of fascination for him as again his covetous gaze reached out and touched her. He could not help noticing how the climbing sun glinted down on her loosened hair and seemed to imbue it with a life all its own. Once, long ago in Sonora, Curragh had seen gold-dust and rock heated in pots and transformed into molten metal. Liquid gold! That just about described— It was then that the first faint warnings of danger penetrated to his senses.

Up in front, alongside the heavily laden wagon, Charlie Dodge had again halted the band, this time to receive news from Walt Tanner, returned from scouting the way ahead. And, as the clattering bustle of men and horses died down and the Conestoga's iron-bound wheels ceased to turn, a new sound charged the early morning air.

The drum-beat of racing hooves struck sharply through the sudden quiet, and men swung quickly in their saddles and reached instinctively for six-guns and rifles. Yet there could scarcely be cause for alarm or even concern, for by the sound of things, no more than two-three riders were headed their way. Curragh it was who first saw the two horsemen when they showed themselves some half-mile or so distant and north of the Trail.

'Only two of 'em,' he called, 'but sounds like there's another couple behind someplace. Now what in hell—?' Those were the last words that Blaze Curragh was destined to utter. For somewhere off to the left a horse had nickered shrilly and at the same instant a rifle barked from behind an upthrust of sage- and mesquite-screened rock. That first bullet, fired with such shocking suddenness and from so unexpected a quarter, struck the horn of Curragh's saddle, ricochetting away harmlessly enough. But a second slug screamed across the Trail even before Curragh could wheel his cavorting mount or pin-point the unseen bushwhacker. He felt little more beyond the shocking impact of a heavy calibre slug slamming into his breast. Just for a moment pain rose like a consuming tongue of fire, and then came darkness black and impenetrable, extinguishing the hurt like a snuffer utterly obliterating a candle-flame.

As the Long Rail men had hoped, Dodge and his gang were indeed caught flat-footed during that opening gambit. Luck as well as timing had played a part, for no one could have foreseen that at this precise moment the outlaw leader would have cause to halt his men and confer. The natural result of such a sudden act had been a general closing up of ranks. Riders who had loafed along in the rear, to bait the captive or feast their eyes, had swiftly transferred their attention ahead.

And Jimmy Yoakum was no slouch in exploiting any such advantage; at once sizing up the position from his rock and brush shelter and realizing that for a while at least the very size of this renegade band was to their own disadvantage.

Grim-visaged, the Texan kid watched the effect of his second shot as it took that nearmost rider in the breast, half-knocking him from the saddle. The bunched outlaws were turning their mounts hard, with the vital need to spread out. Someone began to shout an order, but the words were lost in the urgent rising din of battle.

Too many things were happening simultaneously for Dodge's men to get the measure of this attack in those first decisive moments. No sooner had a dozen of them swung from leather with guns blazing away at the deadly repeating rifle yonder, than the two riders north of the Trail reined in and began pumping lead in a wicked crossfire. Horses squealed and went down and men cursed and Charlie Dodge's voice rose, high-pitched with fury, as he fought to re-establish some kind of control.

3

THE GOLDEN FURY

And then, like bats out of hell, Rebel and Pinto swept round the bend and thundered down into the midst of that mêlée. Dust and gun-smoke drifted over the scene of conflict, aiding the attackers in their brash rescue attempt. Another few seconds only and the outcome might well have been one of bloody tragedy for the Texans. But Yoakum, though bespattered with flying rock splinters and ricochetting bullets, had managed to drop a second man near to the girl. It was Mel who went down, cursing wildly as the bullet struck his leg. Already, Whitey had veered away, slipping the lead rein and no more mindful of the girl now than if she had been a piece of deadwood or a boulder rock.

Tracey had perhaps ten seconds in which to slash through the rope binding the girl's wrists to the saddle and sweep her up and onto his own horse while Pinto emptied a pair of six-shooters into the gang of despoilers. The steady cross-fire which Rede and Toke and Jimmy had been able to pour down, had held death at bay for the Texans;

had enabled the Long Rail foreman to whirl his doubly laden mount and spur away fast, with Pinto hard after him. Pinto with a bullet-slashed shoulder, grimly fighting the waves of giddiness threatening to engulf him.

Behind the brush-covered rocks, Jimmy's carbeen flew from his hands, the stock struck and splintered by a heavy calibre Sharp's slug. Through the curtain of dust and smoke he glimpsed three men spring to their saddles, turning and rowelling their mounts in the direction of the vanishing Tracey and Pinto.

Instinctively Yoakum kicked the useless rifle aside and drew his six-gun, fanning the hammer and slamming his shots into the pursuing trio. In this way, and standing up clear of cover, he achieved three hits. In this way, too, he met his death...

Five-six hundred yards away, Rede Blackmer felt the wind whip past his hat with a tugging force too close for comfort. He loosed off his last shot and shoved the empty Spencer back into its scabbard.

'Tracey's made it, by the looks o' things, Toke,' he yelled. 'Let's quit this neck o' the woods dam' *pronto!*'

Steinhaus jerked his head in acknowledgment, wheeled his mount and waited for Blackmer to come alongside before spurring away from the hail of close-singing lead.

Together they raced back over the same ground they had travelled only minutes before, low in the saddle and swerving a little every few yards in an effort to distract the gun-throwers behind. Just beyond the nearest clumps of brush and scrub oak, they were forced to draw rein. The ponies were lathered up, their breathing laboured, and whilst Toke's gaze moved over the country ahead and parts of the Trail visible from this angle, Rede Blackmer looked back, eyes alert for any indication of pursuit.

'Dadblast it!' Steinhaus muttered. 'Reckon we ain't ever started a shindig like this one before, not even in Ragtown.'

'Nor ain't we ever braced a bunch thet size, Toke. I still cain't figger how we's all in one piece.'

'I ain't so sure about Jimmy!' He shook his head, gaze swivelling back to cover the terrain ahead and to his right. 'Last time I saw him, he was standin' up, blazin' away with a six-gun, looked like. Reckon mebbe he was coverin' Tracey an' Pinto.'

'Yeah. Well, I didn't sight him at all. Mebbe he has gone down an' we won't know yet awhile. But bigawd, Toke! We shore gave them bustards a merry time, didn't we?' He slewed round in the saddle, squinting through the thin haze of sunlit dust. Over a mile away, a bunch of riders had cut loose from the main band and were heading out.

'Six-seven of 'em aim to ride us down, Toke. We gotta push these Long Rail crow-baits plenty hard, clear back to them sandstone bluffs! How's that spavined buck o' yours?'

Steinhaus wiped sweat from his sun-black-ened face, pulled his shorthorn moustache thoughtfully and pushed out a meagre smile. 'He'll make it, Rede, don't you fret. An' them hosses back there cain't be much fresher than ours. Let's git!'

They rode hard, slowed to a walk, and then pushed their labouring ponies to a canter. Not only were they maintaining the distance; they were slowly increasing their lead. Even so, this return journey took twice the time of the outgoing one. It was all of forty-five minutes before they crossed back over the Santa Fé Road near to the mas-sacred freighters. They forced the weary, saline-flecked animals up the rocky slope to the low bluffs, feeling a deep, warm relief at sight of Pinto and Tracey and the girl, yet knowing now with a flat certainty, that the kid had drawn the Ace of Spades in this day's game.

'You bin hit, Pinto!' Rede slid from his streaming horse, laying his gaze on the oldster, who leaned back against a boulder, left arm supported by a sling.

Pinto nodded. 'Slug clean through the shoulder. Tracey jest fixed it – feels like I bin kicked by a two-ton mule!'

Rebel looked from one to other of these hard-eyed men, and Blackmer shook his shaggy head and pulled out sack and papers. 'I reckon the kid ain't comin' back, Tracey. Toke sighted him standin' up, usin' that .44 Colt's gun…'

'Sure.' Steinhaus' eyes slid away to the right, where the girl, white-faced, half-crouched against a low wall. Only by the heaving of her breasts under the torn and faded linsey-woolsey dress and the dark heat smouldering there in her eyes, did she evidence any interest in her surroundings. Her body was still and her tongue silent, and she much reminded Toke of a wounded cougar he had once found lying at the foot of a tree, unable even to crawl, yet alert to every sound and movement, liquid eyes looking out onto its immediate world with angry menace and suspicion; despite its lameness, still deadly enough if a man were to approach within range of those bared fangs!

Right now, he was asking himself the question: *What was so precious about this woman, that Jimmy's life had had to be traded for hers?*

'It's like Rede said, Tracey. We was both too far away an' too goddam busy to see much. But so long as the kid was usin' thet carbeen, he sure kept under cover.' Steinhaus shrugged wide shoulders. 'Mebbe it got over-heated like he feared an' that's why he stashed it an' used his pistol.'

'Looks like them jaspers ain't so eager now.' Rede Blackmer had taken Pinto's glasses from the saddle and had them focussed on a dense tangle of scrub and brush some thousand yards away. 'A bunch of 'em was trailin' us, Tracey,' he elaborated, 'but their hosses ain't in much better shape than ours.'

Rebel nodded and stepped forward, narrowed gaze following the direction Blackmer indicated. 'Looks like they're sheltering in those thickets, Rede, an' I'd say they've had enough taste of Texan lead to make them overly cautious.'

'I reckon yo're right an' likely enough they's figgerin' we got plen'y more men behind us.'

Tracey said, 'They got the advantage in numbers all right, but if they're at all smart, I'll bet this little bunch is only taking a *pasear* before heading back and rejoining the others.'

'I heerd the Military's usin' this road more every day,' Pinto cut in. 'Sure, they'd be chancin' their necks to come after us now the sun's up.'

Rede put a match to his unlit quirly and drew the smoke down with deep appreciation.' They also gotta get that wagon stashed away some place where it cain't be traced.' He paused reflectively. 'Me an' Toke'll hang back a bit, Tracey, an' watch out, when yo're ready to ride.'

'Sure. Pinto's not as spry as he figgers an' I got a termagant to handle!'

Blackmer stared, noticing for the first time the long ragged furrows of dried blood on the ramrod's dust-caked face.

Wonderingly, his glance shifted to the girl and back to Rebel. 'Don't tell me *she–?*'

'Sure I did it, an' I'll do it again – to him or any other man as lays his dirty hands on me!'

She had risen to her feet and the blazing hatred in her face held them all still, more so than her actual words.

'Ain't you got things a little mixed, lady?' Steinhaus was the first to break the dragging silence. He pushed forward and stopped abruptly ten feet away, rocked back on to his bootheels by the expression of utter loathing and contempt on her face. It was there, too, in the dark green eyes and behind that bitter hatred swam fear, stark and primitive.

'We done braced them kidnappers, lady,' he snarled, 'jest so's you could go free an' not be–' He choked on the words and swore softly below his breath. 'Right now,' he told her fiercely, 'one of our men's lyin' out there, down the Trail, dead as mutton, eyes starin' up into the sky! But he won't see those buzzards circlin'–'

'Hold it, Toke!'

Tracey moved across and touched Steinhaus gently on the shoulder. 'We knew the risks we was takin', *amigo,* and – wal, I guess Miss Masterton is pretty sick–'

'Sick am I?' She was poised like a doe encircled by hunters, her feet apart, her arms spread out and pressed against the wall behind. Yellow hair half-curtained her face and cascaded down over bared shoulders. 'Sick am I?' she repeated, and laughed abruptly. 'Mebbe I am! But not the way you mean! Not ill with a fever; jest sick of – of coyotes as call themselves men an' come crawlin' on their bellies for what they can git – like sidewinders in the grass – slippery an' quick an' – an' then changin' all of a sudden, usin' their strength an' power when they find that wiles is no good...' She paused, breathless and panting, and Tracey saw that her fingernails had drawn blood from the palms of her hands.

'Sure. I've seen it, make no mistake, mister. Even some o' them freighters I was travellin' with, wasn't a heap better.' Her red lips curled back, exposing white, even teeth, and though her words were for all, it was Tracey Rebel on whom her glittering gaze remained throughout the tirade. 'Not enough for a man to take himself a wife! No, he's gotta come sneakin'–'

'Listen, Miss Masterton!' Rebel felt suddenly too weary for anger. 'All we're doin' is trying to help you, an' all we know is we mixed in with some outlaw bunch for one reason alone! We heard shots first off, around dawn. Time we got here the fighting was over, but we spotted those raiders way off, headin' south-west along this road. And we saw a woman tied to a saddle—'

'You shore must have powerful good eyes, mister, on account we musta ridden three–four miles to git back here...'

'Bigawd, Tracey!' Blackmer swore. 'We gotta stand an' listen to this hell-cat's foolish talk—?'

Rebel's glance hit him like a physical blow and Rede felt a swift surge of shame that even for a moment his loyalty to Tracey and, therefore, Long Rail should be in doubt.

'She doesn't know the story yet, by a half, boys. There hasn't bin time to tell her we're Texans, trailin' beef to the Arkansaw Valley—'

'So that's your story!' Esther Masterton spat the words out and threw them in Tracey Rebel's face. 'Whoever heard of hazin' cattle from one State to another? Like as not yo're just another such band of pillaging murderers as—'

'Just a few years back Carson drove a flock of over six thousand sheep, clear from Taos to Sacramento. If it can be done with woollies, Miss Masterton, why not cattle?' Rebel swung abruptly on his heel. 'What's that bunch o' riders doin' now, Toke?'

'They done quit, like you figgered, Tracey, but me an' Rede'll still give you a head start if you want.'

'Sure. But keep us in sight an' if you spot anyone, don't tangle with 'em but come a-runnin'! That clear?

'Pinto! You rested up enough to ride, or shall I send the wagon–?'

'Naw!' The Long Rail *segundo* pushed to his feet, clamping his jaws tight as a steel trap against the wave of pain. Rede held the pony while Pinto dragged up into the saddle and sat there a moment, panting heavily. Rebel walked over to the girl and stared down at her, understanding to some extent at least the reasons motivating her extreme attitude.

'We're takin' you back to our camp, Miss Masterton, where you'll be fed an' cared for. No one's goin' to hurt you, but you'll haveta bide with us on the trail till we can find some town or village–'

'Supposin' I – refuse?'

He said, as patiently as he could, 'Far as we could see, and from what little you told me, everyone was killed in your camp, 'ceptin' yoreself. D'you figger we oughta jest leave you here?'

'Mebbe I'd prefer jest that, Mister Tracey!'

'We're ridin' *now,* lady, an' it's up to you

whether you go hawg-tied or of yore own free will!'

She glared back at him, and then all at once it seemed that the fight drained from her completely. Slowly she straightened up from the wall and with a barely perceptible lift of her shoulders, walked beside Rebel to the ground-anchored pony.

From the moment of arriving at the Long Rail camp Esther Masterton's whole demeanour had undergone a bewildering transformation. Gone was the vixen, the termagant, to be replaced by a creature, if sullen, then at least docile and oddly malleable.

At first, Garston and George Mansella and the rest of John Bartlett's trail crew had stared open-mouthed at sight of Tracey with a girl up behind the cantle. But surprise quickly gave way to a rough, practical concern when Pinto half-flopped from his mount.

Food and coffee were dished out and the wounded man attended to before Tracey recounted the story, and long, speculative glances were directed at this Golden Fury who now elected to sit apart from the camp, with maidenly reticence. And though Rebel confined himself to a strictly factual account of the running fight and rescue, the girl's very changed attitude sheered the edge clean off his story. If it had not been for Rede and Toke riding in shortly with their own colourful version, then Zing and the others would likely be figuring their trail boss needed a good rest or a dose of physic!

Rebel turned his head to where the girl reclined against the chuck-wagon's rear wheel, a blanket wrapped tight around her.

'Sure,' he said. 'It all sounds crazy, I know, but she isn't much more'n a kid, I'd say. And you got to remember she must've bin through seven kinds of hell since those outlaws jumped the camp, killing, robbing—'

'You mean,' Zing Garston whispered, 'it – it's mebbe touched her mind?'

Rebel scowled. 'N-no, I don't figger it quite like that. It's jest that she's had what you'd call a bad shock, I guess.' He stopped abruptly and commenced to roll a quirly. 'I cain't forget that Jimmy's out there…'

'Listen, Tracey,' Mansella growled. 'If we was faced with the same kinda thing again, we'd still play it the way you an' Pinto an' the others did, wouldn't we?'

'Sure we would!' It was Blackmer horning in. 'Quit blaming yoreself, Tracey. Jimmy couldn't beat a full house, is all! We—'

'Mebbe so.' Rebel's voice held an unusually sombre tone. 'Pinto might've—'

'Take more'n a slug through the shoulder to lay that bustard flat for any length of time,' Steinhaus grunted, nodding towards the blanket-shrouded *segundo* now sleeping peacefully a few yards away. Mansella, who was not entirely unskilled in such things, had re-dressed Pinto's wound and spooned a stiff dose of laudanum down his throat – enough at least to guarantee the oldster several hours of revitalizing sleep.

Rebel came to his feet, looked at the men across from him. 'I'm headin' back an' find Jimmy…'

Mansella said sharply, 'Let me an' a couple of the boys–'

'It's my chore, George!'

Blackmer placed his coffee cup on the ground and stood up. He looked at Stein-haus and swung his head round to Tracey, bearded jaw thrust out. '*Our* chore, wouldn't you say?'

'Sure.'

''*Stá bueno!* Me an' Toke'll go saddle up then.'

Tracey nodded. 'Who's with the herd, Zing?'

'Bristow an' Mackilvray. Prine an' Lovelace take over at noon.'

'Then listen, boys, an' make sure Bristow and Mac understand. You all keep a sharp eye on the Masterton girl. I'm thinkin' she's a mite too quiet an' docile…'

'What's on yore mind, boss?' Ed Lovelace inquired.

'Damned if I know for sure. But I got a

59

hunch she may try pullin' stakes – any time! Mebbe make some excuse an' jest slip away on the quiet.'

'She'd be shore crazy to do that, Tracey. Alone, on foot, in *this* country?' It was Jim Prine who voiced the scepticism that lay mirrored in every man's eyes.

Rebel hunkered down on his bootheels and his sober glance included each one in turn. He thought back to that dramatic scene on the bluffs, when he had told Toke the girl was sick; how she had scathingly twisted the word's meaning.

'Mebbe she is crazy enough to try it,' he muttered. 'That don't mean she's mad, not by a jugful! But if she did *vamos* and we couldn't pick up the trail…'

Rede and Toke came up, leading four fresh ponies, and Rede handed down the spurs from Tracey's saddle.

'There's another thing,' Rebel added. 'We cain't move on for a coupla days, till we're sure Pinto's wound's healin'. And that bunch of renegades has likely got a hide-out around someplace, mebbe within a few miles.' He buckled on the spurs and moved over to the buckskin Steinhaus was holding and climbed into the saddle.

'You figger they might try somethin', Tracey,' Zing frowned, 'like comin' after the girl?'

'*Quién sabe?* They might if they figgered

they could get away with it. Not jest for the girl, mebbe, but for the sheer hell of it an' punish the jaspers as spoiled their play!'

'Sure. They's a mean enough bunch,' Toke murmured. His eyes went cold as ice. 'We done seen what they did over to that freighters' camp.'

'We'll keep our eyes peeled,' Garston promised, 'but you ain't figgerin' on bein' away long?'

The trail boss shook his head, glancing quickly at the sun. 'Not much after eleven o'clock now. Ought to be back in a coupla hours or so.'

They trotted from camp, Rebel and Blackmer slightly to the fore, Steinhaus following up with the spare horse on a lead rein...

They set no cracking pace. There was still time to reach Yoakum's body before the carrion birds deemed it safe to approach in slow-descending spirals.

A mile from the sandstone bluffs they reined in and built smokes.

Rebel's gaze described an arc over the terrain ahead and to their flanks, but nothing moved except grass and brush stirred by the warm breeze and the dark specks hovering against a backcloth of steel blue to the southwest.

'Me an' Toke had a quick looksee, Tracey,' Blackmer said, 'before followin' you an' Pinto back to camp...'

'We figgered it best to keep quiet until now on account vixens has sharp ears,' Toke finished.

'Bad was it?'

'You can say that seven times over, Tracey boy,' Rede growled. 'Musta bin a score of 'em, mostly men, but five-six wimmen, mebbe. One hombre was still alive – their guide, I'd say, judgin' by the buckskins.'

'Didn't he talk?'

Rede said, 'He only lasted a few minutes, mumbled somethin' about Dodge an' then cashed in his chips.'

'Dodge! That rings a bell,' Tracey said, grim-faced. 'Bartlett mentioned the name when he returned from Colorado. It was jest small talk, for John was too full of this cattle-drive scheme to spare thought on much else.

'I recollect he told of some 'breed called Charlie Dodge operatin' a big gang of cut-throats somewheres along the Santa Fé Road. I guess we didn't know quite what we was doin' bracin' that bunch!'

'Just as well, I reckon, but we picked this up, Tracey.' Rede drew a slim, leather-bound volume from the pocket of his brush-jacket. 'If the yaller-haired girl told you her name was Masterton, then leastways she ain't a liar, I'd say.'

Rebel took the proffered book, seeing it for a selection of Longfellow's works and bearing the title of one of his earlier poems called 'Voices of the Night.' Thoughtfully he flicked the pages back to the fly-leaf, reading aloud the carefully penned inscription.

'"To my dear niece, Esther Masterton, with affection, from her Uncle Tobias Donnell. August 18, 1854. Kansas."' Tracey closed the book and looked up. 'She volunteered the name jest before you both showed up. I asked her several other questions, but she– Whereabouts exactly did you find this, Rede?'

'Near to a wagon which, like all the others, had bin well-nigh stripped of merchandise. Come to think of it, there was an oldster lyin' half under a pile of household stuff and the book was no more'n a yard away. Likely he was this – Tobe feller, you figger?'

'Whether or not,' Rebel answered, dropping the volume into a pocket, 'Esther Masterton's goin' to be mighty grateful when we give her this. What made you tote it back, Rede?'

'Sure I dunno. Books never was my line o' country. Couldn't never *sabe* more'n a few words here an' there.' He paused and dragged smoke into his lungs and stubbed the quirly out on his saddlehorn. 'Knew a minister's daughter once, years back.' He laughed, and Tracey found himself held by the look on Blackmer's swart face.

'Wasn't that the girlie you once told me of down in Bexar?' Toke prompted.

'Yeah. She was no more'n sixteen years, I

reckon, an' – gentle as a kitten. I never knew anythin' so – so soft an' innocent. An' me? That was a big laugh, *amigos*, me fallin' fer her! I was comin' up nineteen an' less'n a year before I killed a card-sharp an' celebrated all in one night down along Ragtown's Red Light quarter...'

'This book,' Tracey said softly. 'It kinda reminded you of the minister's daughter, Rede?'

The puncher nodded his shaggy head, grinning. Just for a few moments, in his rough way, he relived something pure and precious out of the coarse and lusty limbo of his past. 'Sure. Angeline! That was her name an' nothin' else coulda fitted her better. She usta read that kinda stuff an'– For Chrissake! What in hell we settin' here gabbin' for, like hens after a prayer meetin'...'

'Jimmy never was a kid to fret over a few minutes, *amigo,* 'specially not now, an' you rememberin' somethin' like that.' Tracey's glance slid from one to other of his compadres as Blackmer savagely cuffed sweat or something from his eyes. 'She musta bin a fine girl, Rede,' he added and glanced sharply ahead, switching his attention back to present realities.

'Why no buzzards up thar over the wrecked camp?' he asked suddenly. 'I bin tryin' to figger what was wrong...'

'Mebbe someone's found 'em,' Steinhaus

suggested. 'Best not skyline ourselves on them bluffs.'

They rode on at a faster gait, slowing only when they reached the mesquite and rock above the Trail.

Tracey stepped from leather, signalling the others to remain put. They watched him scrutinize the scene carefully and then straighten up and step back.

'Military,' he told them crisply. 'A troop of cavalry and they're sure giving that camp a goin' over.'

'You reckon we owe 'em anythin'?' Rede said.

'No. Nothin' we could tell 'em they cain't soon find out if they want. There's sign in plenty on the road, but I'll bet a month's pay it all peters out soon after the spot where we hit Dodge and his coyotes.

'Best thing we can do is follow Jimmy's trail on the left here. That way we'll be outa sight of the road all the way.'

4

A CHANGE OF FACE

A sudden, nearby noise must have penetrated into her unconsciousness and roused her from a deep, exhausted sleep. Terror sharpened her face and held her limbs rigid as she saw the men yonder. Dark-visaged, powerful-looking men; rough and ill-kempt and most all heavily bearded. She seemed to stop breathing and only her long, narrowed eyes moved at sight of the cartridge belts strapped around their hips and the long pistols jutting from open holsters.

In those first few seconds of shocked awakening, Esther Masterton believed she was in the outlaw camp. Slowly at first, then like a swift flood, recollection swept over her. These men who called themselves Texans – were they any better, she wondered, than the desperadoes who had robbed and killed the freighters – even poor, harmless Uncle Tobe?

She sensed that they were watching her, though often with quick, oblique glances. Through veiled eyes Esther made her own careful survey, recognizing some of the faces now, and suddenly aware that the man,

Tracey, was nowhere in sight. She cast her mind back, remembering how he had ridden out with the other two, shortly after the meal. But why had her eyes searched for him, she thought, except that maybe there had been a – kindness, as well as a strength, in his face?

Yet, though that first panic had loosened its grip on Esther Masterton's mind and body, she trembled still, haunted with nightmare memories.

Inward her thoughts turned and back. Back to Kansas with its deeds of dark violence. She saw her mother, working like a draught horse. She saw the younger kids, hungry, ragged, with gaunt faces and eyes far too bitter and knowing for their age. The vision of Pa was vague. Shiftless, he had come and gone at intervals and then finally quit for good. This was the Kansas-Missouri border; 'Bleeding Kansas,' where slave-holders and anti-slave men were waging a bitter, bloody war. Where hired ruffians burned and plundered houses and barns, ambushing and lynching men, stealing cattle and horses. And even the women were not immune.

Esther's eyes burned, her long mobile lips pressed together with the tightness of a closing door. She must not forget her sister; was it likely she ever would? How could the memory of that terrible night ever be erased from her mind? The five ruffians fresh from a lynching bee. Kitty. The gun she herself had snatched up and fired in a blind passion of fury and grief. The men, white-faced, sick to their bellies, dragging away their dead leader... Afterwards she watched her mother slowly die ... out of shame for what men had done; out of grief for Kitty and because Ma no longer possessed the will to live.

All this had been burned into Esther Masterton. A deep brand that had left its mark. And then her thoughts surged back, and she was contemplating the present and her own immediate future. She had a part to play if she were going to attempt an escape. Sure, the man, Tracey, and the other three had seen her as a wild-cat, first off, and a grey, dismal satisfaction touched her now at thought of the tall Texan's nail-scarred face. But, since quitting the bluffs, she had striven to present a change of face. And this was how it would have to be from now on out. Like an actress, ready to assume a role; each word and gesture, every nuance calculated to convince her audience beyond all doubt.

She rose to her feet, letting the blanket fall away, willing herself to stand there as though unaffected by their glances. She had no way of knowing that between these rough-and-tumble men and Dodge's outlaws there lay a wide ocean of disparity. For a moment Esther closed her eyes, unable to think beyond a certain point; her dress, which in that savage fight had ripped from her shoulders; her hair, loose and unpinned and flowing down in wild disarray. Pride, and the need to play a role, held her from any show of covert haste. She turned and walked the few paces to the wagon-tongue and sat there, grateful at least for the scrap of shade slanting across her face.

She pinned the torn bodice temporarily, and found herself listening to the small noises of a well-ordered camp: the calm rise and fall of voices, the unhurried scuff of boots and the rattle of pots and pants. Occasionally a man's voice would lift sharply and fade, and against these clearer, more identifiable sounds, drifted the soft thudding of cow-ponies in the brush corral.

A fat, red-faced man approached carrying a covered plate. Over his range-rig he wore a greasy apron, tied around his paunch, and purposefully Esther Masterton eased the taut muscles ridging the line of her jaw. Her lips smoothed to form a gentle fullness, and to Chuck Barringer it looked like a smile, so altered was her whole expression. He grinned and held the plate towards her, whipping the cover away with a little flourish.

'Figgered you might be wantin' another bite t'eat, Miz Masterton, seein' as last time you dropped plumb off to sleep.'

'Oh!' Vaguely she remembered that this

man had brought her some food and drink soon after her dazed arrival. 'I guess yo're the cook...?'

'Sure. Chuck Barringer. Bin Long Rail's hash-slinger fer more years'n I care to figger.'

'Long Rail...?' She studied him from beneath lowered lashes, seeing a man of ruddy countenance, whose thickly stubbled jowls quivered with every movement of his head. A man, ageing and running to fat; a man, who, despite his long-standing vocation, still showed in the rope-scarred and knotted hands the stamp of the born stock-tender.

Chuck nodded. 'Long Rail – J.B. That's the outfit's brand. Now then, ma'am, you best eat thet stew while it's good an' hot.'

'Thanks.'

If her reply was brusque, the Long Rail cook seemed not to notice. For the faintest smile lay on her lips as Barrigner awkwardly brushed both large hands over his apron. 'I'll git you some cawfee, *pronto*.'

Esther watched him return to the fire and then hunger welled up inside her, sudden and compelling; a desire so urgent that she closed her mind to all else, until the plate was entirely clean.

When he returned with the coffee she drank some quickly, her eyes still oblique and shaded. 'This Mr Tracey...' she began, and let the words fall away.

Chuck Barringer pushed back his hat and swung his head towards the north .Mention of Rebel had jerked his mind back to Jimmy Yoakum with a sobering abruptness. The brightness ran out of Barringer's face and left it heavy and dull, like clay. He made as though to speak, and saw the three riders as they breasted a grassy ridge. 'Tracey Rebel is the name, ma'am. An' he's ridin' in now, with Rede Blackmer an' Steinhaus.'

Her glance lifted and focussed on the ridge. 'Aren't there four riders?'

'They's four hosses, sure,' he said softly. 'But only three's bein' ridden! Reckon the other one's totin' Jimmy Yoakum. He was kilt when...'

'When they rescued *me* is what yo're goin' to say, isn't it?' The low vibrance in her voice turned Barringer towards her.

'Jimmy was jest comin' up twenty years old,' he said. ''Only a coupla years back Tracey hauled him outa the muck of San Antone; set the kid square on his two feet.' His hands lifted in a small, sad gesture as he moved away.

Esther's voice trailed after him: 'Please tell – Tracey – I – I'd like to see him, after...'

Barringer turned, nodded and continued on towards the cook-fire.

Rebel stood regarding her woodenly, while he rolled up a *cigarrillo*. 'Chuck said you wan'ed to see me.' His voice sounded flat and tired. 'What's the trouble; you still got us all figgered as outlaws?'

'So long as I'm forced to stay in this camp, Mr Rebel, mebbe there's some place private – some place a woman can fix her hair an' dress, an' clean up; or hadn't that occurred to you?'

She wondered if she were over-playing her part and watched for the effect. Yet in this, her first close appraisal of the man, Esther Masterton saw no further than the rough surface; a tall, lean man with angular features accentuated by the thick, black brows and sideburns. She supposed that in contrast to most all the others he was darkly good-looking. And there was a powerful strength in the flat muscles of his body, in the big, sun-burned hands. The realization that her earlier fears had receded stirred within her a vague bewilderment.

He found a match, dragged it along the wagon-side and fired the quirly. 'Sure. I shoulda thought of it.' He stooped and picked up the blankets, nodding towards a single liveoak some twenty yards away. 'Reckon the first thing is to give you some shade, huh?'

She made no protest and accompanied him to the tree and watched him place the blankets down near to the tree's base. He said, 'I'll walk over to the creek with you...'

'Am I still goin' to be watched every minute of the day?' He caught the quick anger that smouldered in her down-drawn eyes and wondered at it. But his own patience was wearing thin, honed down by the events of today; by this girl's mercurial temper, her blatant ingratitude. And less than an hour back he and Rede and Tobe had laid the shrouded body in its shallow trench by the grass verge, an unmarked grave covered by stones.

Maybe, for a brief moment, Esther Masterton did glimpse something beneath the surface; a fleeting shadow in Rebel's eyes perhaps, and she thought with a deep bitterness of how small was Long Rail's plight compared with her own. She said: 'You expect me to be grateful, of course, Mr Rebel. You've–'

'My God, Miss Masterton! It's a bad enough thing–'

Her voice dropped low. 'Sure! You lost one of yore hands, didn't you, an' all you got in exchange is *me!*' She felt shamed as soon as the words were out and he saw it on her face, in her quick breathing and in the unconscious working of her hands.

He said. 'Hold it! There's brush an' scrub in plenty along the creek an' no one's goin' to disturb you. Reckon though you'll be needin' soap an' towel.' He was gone before she could voice a thought, long-reaching strides taking him to a blanket-pile and war-bag near the fire. Presently he returned, leading a saddled pony. He handed her a small, clean towel and a tin of yellow, glutinous-looking substance.

'Lye-soap?'

'All we got,' he said, and caught up the trailing reins and turned about to face her. 'No one goes anywhere near that beef on foot—'

'Is that the real reason yo're escortin' me, mister, or on account I'm not to be trusted?'

He let that go and reined the horse around, lifting Esther to the saddle. She reached down and smoothed her skirts and the sudden stretch of her body opened the pinned bodice from shoulder to breast. She came erect in the saddle and drew the material across, holding it there and sending him a swift, apprehensive glance.

An expression she had not seen before lay in Tracey Rebel's eyes, a still interest which Esther Masterton inevitably misread, and colour stained her cheeks a dark madder.

'Somethin' else I forgot.' He spoke coolly enough, leading the pony out towards the green-fringed creek. 'Mebbe we can rustle you up some clothes...' He hesitated. 'Jimmy's spare denims an' shirt'd fit best if...'

Her gaze remained firmly fixed ahead. 'If what...?'

'Well, I reckon most women don't hanker

74

to sashay around in men's rig.' His mouth quirked faintly and he added. 'But like the soap, I guess it's all we got.' It surprised him that she agreed quickly without demur.

'I'll shore be glad to – to borrow them ... the sooner the better!'

He nodded, though Esther Masterton's eyes were still averted. And, as they passed the makeshift corral, she noted how the horses were tethered and the number of pintos wearing similar markings...

Once, Tracey's glance slanted up to the girl's face, her interest caught by something over to the creek, and in that off-guarded moment, her skin bruised and dust-caked, her hair blowing wild, he glimpsed some of the beauty that lay in the composed features, and shone from the depths of sage-green eyes, clear now as a rain-washed sky.

When they skirted the grazing herd, Esther inclined her head. 'They look right peaceful enough, save for them flashing horns.'

'Yeah.' He spoke dryly. 'But I guess you never saw them critturs stampede.'

Near to the creek he handed her down and indicated the brush thickets and scrub growing in tangled profusion.

She watched him from a few paces away. 'You figgerin' on doin' this every time I want to clean up?'

He said mildly, 'Anythin' could happen, 'specially if you try runnin' off...'

'Ah! So I *am* a prisoner, after all! Why didn't you–?'

'Only for yore own protection,' he said quickly. 'There's plen'y Injuns around an'–'

'We had brushes with Injuns both sides o' the Arkansaw,' she retorted. 'They did us a sight less harm than yore white men!'

'Mebbe so. But Dodge, the man who attacked yore freighter camp is more'n half Arapaho, I bin told.'

Her eyes slanted on him, quick to fill with suspicion. 'How do *you* know who those men were?'

He built a smoke, lighted it before answering. 'Blackmer and Steinhaus searched the camp…' He shook his head. 'Only the scout was alive. An' he only lasted long enough to tell Rede Blackmer.' He withdrew the book and handed it to her. 'Rede found it an' figgered you might like it back.'

She was suddenly still and quiet, unsure of herself, and he said, 'You give me yore word, Miss Masterton, not to *vamos*, mebbe you can use one o' the spare hosses.'

'Why, thanks.' She nodded, her words slow-spoken and her voice sweet and thick like molasses.

'I'll tell the men, so whoever's duty-wrangler can fix it.' He nodded towards the paint. 'These cow ponies are tough as rawhide. Better tie the reins real secure. Then–'

'Sure. When I'm through I'll bring it right

back to the corral.' She turned quickly for fear of what he might read in her face...

Well, Tracey Rebel had done as he had promised, Esther reflected, but that would not weaken her resolve to escape! She sat on the blanket roll beneath the liveoak's shade. She wore the wool shirt and the shrunken denims that he had left there for her. And more, he had found a scuffed pair of half-boots and a low-crowned sombrero which would not be too large with her hair piled high. At this angle she was partly hidden from the crew in camp, and likely, for a while, she was not in their minds.

She saw them as hard-eyed men. Laconic and crude in their off-guard moments, and she thought to herself: 'No. I'm not mistaken, and I'd be fool-crazy to stay! There's worse hazards than hostile country.'

Esther was beginning to regard the clothes Tracey had found her with mixed feelings, for shirt and denims fitted too tightly either for comfort of body or mind.

She stood up and began moving in and around the camp, occasionally exchanging words with one or two of the men; sometimes a brief smile and an offer to help. It was not easy, this path she had to tread. Some of them, like Steinhaus and Pinto, had formed their opinions right from the start – prejudices now deeply rooted in every tough fibre of their beings. The most she could hope for was a partial victory, lulling suspicion to a point where most of them might start to accept her. But it meant maintaining this newly acquired veneer of hers all the while; and it was a shield deflecting the thrusts of overstrong glances. For in them Esther Masterton read only the primitive stirrings of men too long denied the sight of women. How could she know that for all the wildness of their life, these Texan cowboys had their distinct code of chivalry and honour; that a clear line of demarcation lay chalked in their minds?

Yet she learned several important details concerning general routine, and discovered that on account of Pinto's wound, camp would not be broken until the dawn after tomorrow.

Daylight was fading when she returned from the creek. She turned the pony over to Bill Haycock and walked back towards the camp. Tracey came up from the far side of the corral, more sure about her now.

She heard the scuff of boots and turned, slowing to a halt. In the pale, violet dusk her eyes were very dark and watchful, and he had an idea that they were shaded with a further anxiety.

'Mr Rebel...'

'What is it, Miss Masterton?' he inquired, and rolled up a *cigarrillo*. She was a tall woman, he realised, more appreciably now, in the high-heeled Justins. Nor could Tracey fail to observe the full-rounded symmetry of her figure, so thoroughly accentuated. In his quick haste to find substitute clothing for the damaged dress, he had seemingly made matters worse. But the garment *could* have been repaired, in some fashion, and he found himself wondering half-seriously, if this was her indirect way of showing her thanks.

She spoke in a low voice, her eyes on the bustling camp. 'They told me you – you wouldn't be drivin' on till day after tomorrow, at the earliest?'

'Sure.' He drew on the lighted quirly. The tang of tobacco drifted away on the breeze, and for a moment the scent of her golden hair filled his nostrils. 'Mansella is watchin' Pinto's wound. It's doin' fine, but we decided to stay here another day... An' it gives us time to talk about you, Miss Masterton...'

She said quickly, 'In what way?'

'We gotta set you down someplace, where you'll be safe. Where you can–'

'Oh!' Her breath rushed out like a sighing wind and at once he was reminded of what this day must have cost her.

'We'll discuss it tomorrow.' He touched her arm. 'Right now you need a good meal an' plenty of sleep.'

She nodded and swung in beside him. Resolutely her mind shut against the thin whisper that this man at least was not of the breed of ruffians like Dodge, nor those along the Kansas-Missouri border whose depredations were still leaving a trail of misery and shame. So! Let Long Rail discover if it were as easy to corral a woman against her will as to rope and brand a wild maverick...

Night moved away to the edge of beyond and another dawn flooded the land. For Esther Masterton, carefully observant, camp routine became a familiar pattern. Even through the starlit hours she had roused herself at intervals, watching and listening for the night guards. And almost was she sure that Rebel and the man Blackmer had remained alert in the darkness beyond the fire's glow. Once she had caught the gleam of a polished rifle barrel and the low murmur of voices. Had they elected to guard the camp because of her, she wondered, or as a safeguard against any possible reprisals by Dodge?

The day would run its course faster, Esther reflected now, if she filled the hours with work. She cast around and began tackling one or two light chores as unobtrusively as possible, trying especially to avoid the irascible Pinto and the hostile-seeming Steinhaus.

She searched for sagebrush and greasewood and added each armful to the pile of kindling near the mess fire. Later she found a few dirty cookpots which Barringer had left. Esther scrubbed them with sand until they shone, and suddenly she had had her fill. She straightened up, mildly surprised that except for three punchers repairing bridles the camp was virtually deserted.

When she reached the corral, Haycock had a pony ready, and Esther flashed him a smile and went into the saddle with an easy sureness and headed out for the creek. Close to some scrub oak she reined in and made her long and careful study of this spot before turning left into the thicket. Here again she surveyed the ground and vegetation, memorizing details and gauging distance and direction to the water's edge...

It was mid-afternoon before he came looking for her. She leaned back against the tree, watching his approach through dark lashes.

He said quickly, 'Seems like you bin puttin' in some real hard work around the camp. *Gracias.*'

She straightened her shoulders and just for a moment a warmth touched her face. It was like glimpsing a distant camp fire at night, Tracey thought, or a pale gleam of light from a friendly cabin.

He said, 'Mind if I sit down?'

She nodded and her glance slid to the

81

rough sketchmap he held, and when she said, 'Mebbe you got my future all mapped out there?' the words came at him with a faint edge.

He found her swift change of moods difficult of understanding, and he said, 'Look, Miss Masterton! You got any kinsfolk back in Kansas, anyone at all you could–?'

She shook her head even before he had finished, her eyes flecked now with a kind of angry fear. 'Kansas! I don't ever wanta see that land again! Why you figger Uncle Tobe an' me lit out with them freighters? No! Better by far I go on to Santa Fé.'

'You know someone there, mebbe?'

She turned aside with a slight movement of her arms, an eloquent gesture of resignation. 'In any event, what's the use? They – they stole everythin' from the wagons, didn't they? All I got, mister, is a torn dress an' this – this rig-out you fixed me with. How–?'

A quick impatience roughened Tracey Rebel's face. 'We can raise the *dinero;* that's not the problem…' He turned to the map. 'Mebbe Fort Maya's the best bet. 'Cordin' to this, it lies some fifty-sixty miles to the north. Me an' Rede would break away from the herd an' see you safe…'

'What else is there?' she asked, and suddenly realized there was no point in fighting Rebel and his ideas. Let him figure she was

82

gentled, ready to respond to rein and spur. 'Willow Creek,' she said softly, answering her own question, 'I only just remembered the place an' where it is.' She paused a moment before adding, 'Uncle Tobe an' Wishart talked of it, a new settlement bein' built–'

'Maxwell! Isn't that the man...?'

'Why, sure.' She looked at him in frowning surprise. 'Leastways I think they mentioned a Mr Maxwell – something about a big stretch of land – oh, I guess mebbe over a million acres!'

'The Maxwell Grant,' Tracey recalled. 'Yeah. Ranchin', buildin' new towns...'

Esther nodded. 'Plenty jobs goin', I reckon – for saloon girls!' She was instantly repentant, quick to dispel his doubts with a smiling headshake and reassuring words. 'I guess I was joshin', is all. The fact is, this place is not jest a frontier settlement of saloons an' tents. Way I heard it, men are bringin' their wives an' children.'

'Are you willing we should take you there – look the place over? Mebbe we could even get to see this Maxwell hombre...'

She nodded slowly, and her face in profile seemed to express a complete and sober agreement...

5

ESCAPE BY NIGHT

They had ceased to watch her now, she was sure; the more so since her talk with Tracey. The camp buzzed with the kind of methodical activity that precedes a dawn push.

Esther glanced at the westward sun and judged the time at around five o'clock. She stood up and walked leisurely towards the corral where Mansella was rubbing down a pony. He looked up and nodded. She could have wished Bill Haycock was on duty here, but she concealed such thoughts behind an amiable expression. She had to admit that Mansella was no slouch at his job; she told him so, softly, and had her immediate reward in the dull flush of pleasure in his swart face.

He could scarcely have taken more than thirty-forty seconds to bridle and saddle the paint. And sweating a little, he held the cheek-strap and admired the way she stepped into leather. Esther's glance touched him and moved onto the camp. 'They're dishing out fresh coffee, if you fancy a drink.'

He grinned. 'I could use a cup, sure. But...'

She said easily, 'I'll bring the horse back an' tether it – whether yo're here or not. That's a promise.'

She rode through the narrow opening at an unhurried gait and presently turned in the saddle. Mansella was walking towards the camp, and with a quick shudder of relief Esther Masterton put her mount to a fast trot.

The moment that she reached the creek she turned in to the dense evergreen thicket. She swung from the saddle and firmly secured the reins to a thick stem. Then she began to thread her way back to the more open ground. No doubt that luck was helping her now, Esther thought. There had been five or six pintos, all with similar roan and white markings, and Mansella had slapped saddle and bridle onto one of them! And, unless he were suspicious, it was unlikely he would closely inspect them, especially if she…

Her heart beat faster as she set out to make the return journey on foot. Each step was premeditated in that she held herself ready to drop flat behind the nearest sage bush at a moment's notice. All the while her narrowed gaze remained on the men moving around the wagon and camp fire some quarter mile distant. Any one of them might turn and see her and wonder.

But her luck still held, and she reached the

brush corral feeling a swift surge of triumph and stepped quickly to the pinto she had selected as the ringer.

The animal was held by sidelines, and to Esther, working with feverish haste, the knots seemed to possess an evil resistance. Presently she had the ropes free and led the pony to the spot where her own mount had been tethered. She secured it to the staking pin, using a rope halter.

A few minutes later she was speaking to Mansella. 'I tethered the pony,' she smiled, 'an' removed saddle an' bridle.'

'You did? Say, ma'am, you shore hadn't any need to go luggin' saddles around...'

'It was no trouble.' She turned away and George Mansella grinned and tromped back to the horses.

It seemed to the girl lying in her blankets, that Rebel and Blackmer and Steinhaus would never turn in for the night.

They had been hunkered down near the fire for an interminable period and their voices droned across the scented night air with a deadly monotony which threatened to dull her brain. Yet her senses were sharp as an animal's, instinctively keened to the night.

Sprawled full length on the ground beneath her coverings, Esther registered the soft slow drum of hooves even before the trio of men at the fire. She remained quite still, head slightly raised, nostrils dilated wide, and the sudden thought that perhaps after all, Dodge was closing in to attack, drew sweat from her face and arms.

But Tracey and the others were still clearly silhouetted against the camp fire's glow. They stood now, relaxed and easy, as the rider shaped up out of the night and climbed stiffly from the saddle. It was Lovelace.

She was angry with herself for having overlooked, even momentarily, that here was something no more alarming than normal guard routine; yet significantly the fulcrum on which her escape plan rested.

Her gaze shifted from one to other of the men while she waited out the dragging minutes with breathless impatience.

Steinhaus had at last bedded down, and Rebel and Blackmer moved away, two black shapes quickly swallowed into the shadows. In a short while she heard the whisper of hoofbeats, this time slowly fading into the distance, and she knew that Tracey and Rede were heading for the herd.

When Mackilvray rode in, he led both horses to the corral, presently joining his partner Lovelace in a last cup of coffee. It was not long before both men crawled wearily into their blankets.

The time, Esther guessed, was around ten-thirty. Nearly two hours and a half before either Blackmer or Tracey Rebel would come riding back to waken their reliefs! Yet, if she could make a real clean break, then likely enough it would not be discovered before dawn. She would have best part of the night in which to put the miles between herself and these rough-and-tumble Texas men!

Quickly Esther withdrew the meat and bread she had purloined, using the discarded dress to wrap the food into a compact bundle.

In the darkness she groped around for the brush and deadwood which she had gathered at intervals throughout the day, and thrust them underneath the top blanket to create the necessary illusion. She moved away, paused long enough to further adjust the blanketed shape, and began to edge away on hands and knees. Every few moments she stopped to listen carefully; but heard only the soft night voices of the land and the more raucous man-made snores, yonder.

It was a painfully laborious business crawling along in this fashion, and she set her teeth together, contemptuous of the sharp stones and thorn splinters in the visualization of tougher hardships to come.

Once clear of the sleeping camp, she slowly straightened up, and as she approached the corral, slackened her pace, pausing between each tentative step, and mindful more of the cavvy than of the sleeping Mansella.

Without warning one of the animals nickered shrilly, just as the girl began to draw away from the brush and rope enclosure. She froze at once, probing the night, hearing only the sledge-hammer pounding in her breast. Still she waited, but beyond a muffled stamping of hooves, no further sound disturbed the night, and gradually she began moving forward again, lengthening her stride, walking quickly and steadily until the creek's thick brush and scrub growth loomed up ahead. Once again it became necessary to tread warily, to avoid outstretched thorns and foliage and to orient her position.

She stumbled on towards the thicket, catching a foot in some trailing vine and sprawling full length onto the ground with a force that slammed the breath from her body. For seconds on end she fought with bitter stubbornness to feed air into her lungs, and even when the breathing became easier she remained lying there, suddenly confronted by a deep uncertainty. Slowly, Esther shook her head and hauled herself upright. She caught up the bundle of food before veering to the left and plunging into the dense blackness of the thicket.

She had not doubted that the pony would still be there, tied as she had left it. But its whinny of pleasure and the eager thrusting of its soft nose, brought a lump to the girl's throat. Forage in plenty was there within reach, but for long hours since afternoon it had gone without water, tantalized by the cool scent of the creek. She struggled over the knotted reins, managing at last to free the animal and maintain a hold as it lunged to the water's edge and drank long and deep. Seeing it like this prompted Esther Masterton to examine the canteen, finding it almost empty.

She hurriedly slid the food package into a saddle pocket and filled the canteen. In another moment she was in the stirrups and putting her mount to the creek and searching the way ahead with only the stars for compass and light.

The breeze strengthened and became a wind, singing its mournful song through the trees and grass. Clouds drove in from the north-west and drew an ever-widening blanket across the stars. The shapes of trees and rocks and brush were no longer as sharply etched as before and gradually became merged into the deepening background.

She sat well forward in the saddle, eyes straining to pierce the almost ink blackness. It was not feasible to travel above a walking gait, and she began to lose all sense of direction.

The wind veered sharply, striking through her clothes with a gusty, whipping force. In the ensuing lull, the air seemed all at once oppressive, and as she drew rein a series of vivid flashes burst across the sky, illuminating the terrain and then leaving it seemingly darker than before. She smothered her own sudden panic and strove to pacify the horse.

Thunder rolled from the massed clouds and echoed away into the distance like volleys from a giant cannon. And again the lightning flooded down with seering brilliance and Esther saw the phosphorescent glow dance and bob along the sharp-pointed horns of cattle.

For an infinitesimal moment of time she thought that some trick of the storm had created this illusion, this strange kind of mirage in which lay pictured the gleaming horns and nebulous shapes of countless wild-eyed cattle. Yet to the Long Rail pony, danger physical and absolute threatened, and it took all of her skill and strength to force its head back, holding it in submission on a short-iron-hard rein.

Some at least of the animal's urgent fear communicated itself to Esther Masterton, and instinctively she associated the renewed thunder with that terrifying mirage a moment ago. The rumbling was more steady and continuous; no more did it shake the heavens, but instead trembled the very ground under her.

It could only be the thunder of galloping hooves, she realized; the fast-mounting roar of a panic-stricken herd at full run!

Nearer to hand came the sharper, staccatoed rataplan of shod hooves and riders swept out of the night and were suddenly rendered clear and recognizable in the bright storm flashes. She saw the cattle again, a dark sea of hurtling shapes, plunging across the creek and through the tangled underbrush, and she saw the grim, glistening faces of men and the guns in their hands before blackness descended again to erase the picture and leave only a cacophony of noise in this terror-filled night.

But there were smaller flashes, yellow-orange in colour, and now Esther heard those blazing guns and at once she neck-reined her sweating horse with unthinking cruelty, yet hesitant to ride until the lightning came again.

The stampede's booming roar reached its zenith and began to lessen. Again the crack of guns stabbed the night in a renewed flurry of action, and horsemen pounded by and abruptly hauled up, their voices high-pitched and strident in her ears. Her hands tightened on the reins in a sudden desperate resolve.

The thundering herd had passed her by, but danger, perhaps even death, still rode the night in the shape of armed men. They were not Long Rail, of that she was sure; not the men she had seen in the light of those first flashes. Yet...

This time the land was lit as clear as day. The brilliance lasted for seconds on end, and Esther turned in the saddle and saw the men close up and knew that her worst fears had materialized out of the stormy night.

'*Bigawd! It's the yaller-haired witch...*'

Dodge's voice, thin and cruel, came at her like a whiplash, causing her to recoil in the saddle. In those few nightmare moments, Esther glimpsed others of the bunch whose evil faces were all too familiar. And then, with shocking violence, rain poured down from the laden clouds. Blackness shut down like a solid wall, obscuring everything from sight. Even the sounds of shouting men and moving horses were beaten back and lost in the flash flood. Wildly, Esther Masterton kicked her pony into action and turned and plunged headlong into the night.

She had no clear thought or feeling in her, beyond a fearful knowledge that escape from these men was imperative, whatever the outcome.

For a long while she remained half-numbed, senses dulled by the cold, lashing rain and the impenetrable blackness all around...

The pony was struggling to retain a foothold on ground turned to a sea of running mud. It's breathing was painfully laboured and every instinct in the animal cried out to halt and turn its rump to the storm. Somehow the girl kept it going, refusing to ease the pressure until it stumbled and broke stride, slithering to a halt on the waterlogged ground.

Esther hauled on the reins, setting the weight of her body far back in the saddle. It was an instinctive reaction, as quick as the flash storm itself. She had no time even to realize that the torrent had ceased as suddenly as though shut off by a faucet. The paint recovered, floundered and slipped again. But Esther's quick counter-measures saved it from going down and herself from being thrown.

She sat still for a while, feeling the water stream down her shivering body, slowly becoming aware once more of the world around her. The blackness had lifted perceptibly and the sounds of night began to stir softly again over the storm-drenched land.

She groped in the saddle pocket and found that despite the beating rain her store of food was not spoiled. She remained in the saddle, chewing some of the bread and jerked beef, trying to clear her mind.

Already the clouds were thinning fast and she could make out their ragged edges as they scudded away. Stars glistened against the clearing sky, and she recalled that though the wind had veered it had first whipped in from the north-west. It took a few moments for her to keen it, feeling it blow softer now on to her left cheek. It seemed unbelievable at first, that chance or blind instinct must have guided them through the night *in the right direction!*

Impulsively her hand stretched out and patted the drooping neck, and in the brightening starlight she saw the lip of a deep ravine no more than a few yards to her right. Gently, hardly daring to breathe, she reined away from the ravine and began to travel on at a slow walk. An hour or so later she drew her feet from the stirrups and swung a leg over the saddle horn, hitting the soggy ground with a stiff-legged jolt. She kept a hold on the reins and ploughed along beside the animal, and felt weighted down by a deep and utter weariness.

Slowly, Esther Masterton became aware that the going was harder underfoot; that her boots were no longer dragging mud and only at wide intervals were the shallow rock depressions water-filled. The paint stopped to drink from one of these, and Esther leaned against the saddle and was instantly asleep on her feet. When the pony scented out some forage sprouting from a rock fissure it swung its head and moved sharply away, sending the girl sprawling to her knees. Bruised and shaken, she came up from the unyielding ground, tears welling in her eyes. Quite suddenly she threw back her head and laughed aloud, wringing a kind of sour humour from this whole anti-climax.

She moved across and caught up the reins, knowing that the Long Rail pony was as tuckered out as herself; knowing, too, that they could not stop yet. This time it took her three attempts before she finally hit the saddle. Even to turn and search her back trail was becoming too much of a mental and physical effort. A long time later she felt the pony's hooves strike grass, firm and dry, and the rocky ground lay behind. Wearily she veered slightly and headed due north into rising country.

A pearl-grey dawn streaked the eastern sky and steadily the world brightened until the first gleam of sunlight stabbed a new-washed bowl of Heaven.

Esther willed herself to pull in and slide from leather in a brushy bowl. It was a good place to camp – or hide – protected by thick timber, mesquite and piñon. She could do no more than loosen cinches and tie the reins to a stout brush stem. Her eyes were already closed as she dropped down onto the tawny grass and straightway drifted into the deep sleep of exhaustion.

6

LONG RAIL PUSHES ON

In the late forenoon Garston and Starett returned on hard-pushed mounts. Bleak, red-rimmed eyes watched the two riders with a dismal interest. No one spoke except Rebel, and on his face was the granite look of a man who has lately learned a hard lesson. He said, 'Any luck, Zing?'

Garston nodded and managed a tight grin, and a ripple of interest quickened throughout the camp.

He said, 'Me an' Jed's found most of 'em, Tracey. Three-four bunches, 'bout five miles to the east–'

'How many, Zing, for God's sake?'

They unshipped from leather and dropped the reins. Haycock, coming in from the corral, stepped across towards the horses.

'Most all of 'em.' Garston pushed back his hat, wiped sweat and dust from his seamed face. 'Reckon there's no more'n a coupla dozen carcasses strewn around. Some was trampled, some fell an' jest natcherally busted their necks.'

Jed Starett spat a thin stream of juice into

the fire and nodded. 'They's plumb worn down, Tracey, but once we git them hazed back on this grass...' He squatted down on one of the tarps spread over the sodden ground and Tracey, grinning, turned his head towards the wagon and called, 'Chuck! How many bottles of corn we got left?'

Barringer did not have to check supplies to answer, 'Four pints, I guess, but George says—'

'To hell with Mansella! Open a couple, Chuck. These buzzards deserve it. 'Sides which, we got somethin' to celebrate, I reckon!'

'Buzzards!' Zing Garston nodded soberly. 'Sometimes them jackal birds can help plen'y.' He dropped onto the tarp alongside Starett and rolled up a quirly and sent his glance round and back to Rebel. 'It looked kinda hopeless fust off, Tracey. Jest like the rest o' you, we couldn't pick up any trail. Everythin' washed out—'

'Only steers across the creek,' Jed put in, 'was mostly dead o' lead poisoning from them Dodge killers ... yeah, an' we found one o' the bustards too!'

Rede Blackmer's shining face pushed forward. 'You mean we really kilt one o' them sneakin' coyotes all in the dark?'

Garston shook his head. 'This hombre was kicked to death, Rede. Mebbe some o' the others was hit, but we didn't figger on lookin' on account Jed spotted them buzzards far over to the east. We shore travelled to git there.'

Bill Haycock looked at the drooping ponies. He said drily, 'Sure you did,' and led them towards the corral.

Garston dragged on the quirly. 'You can reckon on most o' fourteen hun'ed head, Tracey; mebbe more and in fair shape. They's bunched in a series o' grassy draws…'

Chuck came over carrying a large pastry board laden with tin cups, each holding its measure of liquor. Rope-burned hands reached out and every man gulped down his drink with an undeviating singleness of purpose.

Rebel tossed aside his empty cup and wiped his mouth. 'It's not bin any cinch pushin' that beef herd,' he growled. 'An' inside the last forty-eight hours we had it pretty rough!' He put a match to the quirly he had fashioned and added quietly, 'But 'cept for Jimmy an' Pinto's arm, we bin goddam lucky this far.'

They nodded; some packed and lit stubby pipes. This was a moment snatched for relaxation, before the big effort. Most of all these rawhide men had been a part of the Long Rail outfit from the beginning. They knew no other god, and their loyalty, like a simple faith, lay deep and unquestioning. Men like Mackilvray and Prine and even

Garston, might still be sceptical about driving cattle a thousand miles through uncertain country. But Bartlett was prepared to risk his beef, and Tracey, eager to blaze the trail, and the crew had nodded and got to figuring out how much *dinero* they would have to spend by the end of the drive.

A hard breed of men, born to a hard existence. Rough and prideful and often quick to violence over some fancied insult; yet as often unashamedly moved to tears by the memory of a woman's soft voice and gentle smile.

They sweated from dawn to dusk six days a week and more, cussing the work they knew best, for forty a month and all found; living as close to the sun-cured grass and earth and scented sage as any man could. There were those in this bunch, Rebel knew, whose fathers and elder brothers had fought at the Alamo and at San Jacinto to win for Texas her independence...

Will Fourche, a chunky roan-haired man, said quietly, 'When do we start in hazin' them critturs back, Tracey?'

Pinto, squatting on his saddle, nursing his injured arm, called, 'Here's Toke an' Prine comin' in!'

'All right then, let's wait 'n hear what they got to say. If we can be sure Dodge isn't planning another Fourth o' July...'

Glances swung to the north, and a mile

away Prine's arm went up. Rede Blackmer's deep-throated voice rumbled its way around the camp. 'Looks like they got news of Dodge, mebbe.'

Tracey nodded, and shortly, with a wild 'Hurrah,' Prine and Steinhaus spurred their bespattered mounts forward in a last-minute run. They hauled up at the camp in a flurry of outflung mud and threw themselves from saddles.

'They gone to ground for sure!' Toke spat the words out. 'Like a pack o' sneakin' coyotes. But that ain't any wonder with the Trail alive—'

'Sure,' Prine said. 'Posses bustin out, an' plen'y cavalry. Why, Tracey, some o' them bluecoats was ridin' like Injuns – carbeens acrost their saddles!'

'Hey!' Steinhaus was sniffing the air like a hound on a scene. 'Who in hell's bin bathin' in red-eye?'

'Hold it, Toke! You an' Jim both, an 'listen! *We* got news, too!' Tracey nodded to Garston and Starett. 'Those two helions has run down the herd, over to the east aways, an' most of all 'em's alive—'

'God love us, Tracey! That's the shore finest news we had— But what of that Golden Hellcat an' where's she...?'

'No sign,' Rebel said and stood up, his gaze traversing the crew. 'We can talk about the girl later. Right now the beef's our main concern.' He singled out six riders: Garston, Bristow, Fourche, Mackilvray, Starett and Mansella. 'We-all ride,' he told them. 'Pinto, Rede an' the others'll look out for the camp.'

Lovelace said, 'I'll take a look at the hosses,' and climbed aboard Prine's mount. He caught up Toke's pony and trailed towards the corral.

'You gonna manage it, Tracey,' Pinto frowned, 'jest the seven o' you?'

'Sure.' Rebel looked up at the sky and then swung his gaze across to Barringer. 'Mebbe we'd do better to eat first.'

'That's what I figgered.' Pinto got to his feet and threaded his slow way through gear and blanket rolls towards the chuck-wagon. Halfway he turned and added, 'You better git them critturs back an' bedded down before dark.'

Tracey nodded – watching the oldster as he started alternately threatening and cajoling Chuck to rustle up seven dinners *pronto*. He smiled and turned back to the men moving about the camp. Some were cleaning pistols and feeding in fresh loads, and Prine was headed out after Lovelace to help saddle the horses.

Surprise stirred Tracey then, as he found himself thinking, not of the trail herd, but of a yellow-haired girl riding alone, at the mercy of this hostile country...

They jogged out of camp at a sparing gait and splashed through the swollen creek, Garston and Starett pointing the way. Wind travelled in from the west, drying out a land already firming under eight hours of sun.

When Long Rail pulled in to rest their mounts, Rebel's head lifted to the wet scent of earth and sun-cured grass and the herb-sweetness of sage. In this land, he thought, lay an enduring primitive beauty. It was there in the vast stretches of plain and desert and grassy mesas; in the lofty mountains purpled by distance. It drifted, too, along these aromatic winds like beauty's fragrant breath.

He turned from such wayward flights of fancy, thinking of this grass, the like of which many a Texan had not seen before – grass on which the Long Rail beef had thrived so well.

'You set, Tracey?' It was the sober-faced Zing who brought him back to earth, eyes alert and watchful on the ramrod's face, and Rebel nodded quickly, touching spurs to his mount, heading out with a suddenness that caught them flat-footed.

'He was thinkin' of that girl,' Mackilvray murmured. 'It was in his face.'

'Better not say that loud.' Garston threw the words at Mackilvray softly, and waved the riders along. Twice more Long Rail halted briefly, saving their mounts for the work ahead. They reached country dry and untouched by the storm. Dust rose like a shimmering vapour on the air, slow to move until suddenly caught and whipped into spirals by the lifting wind.

Before them, in an empty-seeming land, the grassy trail spread wide in a series of gentle undulations. It was easier now to understand how the herd had rampaged through to the brushy draws beyond, and had escaped destruction even through the darkness. There were few immediate obstructions save for a small rock formation yonder, and it was here where most of the broken remains lay.

Above the clatter of hooves came the bawling of cattle disturbed or apprehensive, and Rebel eased his mount and called, 'Zing! No turkeys!'

Garston said quickly, 'Like the freighter-camp! That what yo're figgerin'?'

'Yeah.' His gaze swept the sky and the rocks and brush, and suddenly he made his signal, bringing the Long Rail riders to a sharp halt. His eyes were on the piñon-dotted heights to the right.

He said calmly, 'We got company, boys. Get yore carbeens out slow an' easy an' spread out some. Five-six Injuns atop those bluffs.'

They might have reined in to rest and smoke, for their movements were unhurried and natural. One-handedly, Starett neck-reined his mount, sidestepping a pace or two; drawing rifle from scabbard under cover of the pony's arching neck.

Rebel's eyes didn't shift, but he felt and heard the men move around him and his own hand slid to the Spencer's stock.

'Five, ain't it, Tracey?' Will Fourche said from behind. 'Far as can be seen.'

'Yeah.' He had the Spencer clear now and still the Indians made no move. 'But there could be *fifty*-five or more, back o' them rocks...' A horse nickered and the cry was repeated. The Long Rail ponies flicked their ears forward, whinnying softly, their muzzles probing for a scent which the down wind denied them.

Tracey called to the rearmost rider. 'Bristow! Keep yore eyes on our back trail–'

'*Look!*' Jed Starett's exclamation drew quick attention. 'They're pullin' out! You figger we should rush those rocks?'

Rebel, too, had caught that flashing movement of dark-skinned bodies, and he said, 'Hold it, Jed!' and slid from the saddle, carbeen in hand.

He indicated a narrow pathway in the piñon-stippled rock and called, 'Watch it, boys, till we see where we're goin'.' He covered the intervening stretch at a dead run and began to climb.

Fourche eased his mount in alongside

Garston and pointed. 'Along the edge o' that draw, Zing! Looks like a gap in the rock. Lemme cover him from there?'

Garston's glance reached out and his heavy face creased for a cautious moment of doubt. 'All right, Will, but–'

Fourche drew away and spurred his pony to a full gallop over the half-mile or so of grassy trail.

Rebel, nearing the summit, swung his head and looked down and made his quick assessment of Will's intention. Then he turned and climbed the remaining few yards to the top. Brush and tufted grass provided an adequate screen so long as a man kept down, and Rebel wormed his way over the rim rock, hindered both by rifle and by the long-rowelled spurs.

From way below the voice of Fourche sailed upwards in a thin, unexcited call, and like an answering signal came the solid rumble of hooves, a sudden, sharp-thrown noise magnified by some trick of wind or echo.

Rebel lifted up and saw the ledge from where the Indians had watched. He took the small risk and skylined himself, and a smile crossed his face, for all the precautions taken.

There were six of them and they travelled at an easy lope, neither dawdling nor fleeing. One rider led a spare cayuse, heavily laden.

The rearmost Ute reined around sharply and stood motionless, watching; and against his better judgment Tracey felt a grudging kind of admiration.

He shook his head. These Utes and Apaches could be wickedly cruel. Maybe there would be no room for any such tolerance of feeling if Long Rail had ridden into a big war party. 'Well,' he thought, 'let them have the butchered steer,' and considered it was a cheap price to pay under the circumstances...

Long Rail sweated as the breeze lessened and died in the afternoon heat. Yet they knew that this job was easy compared to combing the brakes along the Nueces. These grassy, brush-rimmed draws were little more than a series of shallow basins, sufficient to hold a run-down herd quiet until thirst should drive them out.

The first score or so of creatures choused back onto the trail were quickly bunched into a spearhead. Sure-footed ponies responded to each flick of the rein, each touch of knee or spur, with an instant action. Singly, or in small groups, the longhorns streamed out and merged into the moving, lengthening column.

In brief moments between turning back a steer into line, or riding from point to flank, Rebel studied their condition, finding it better than he had dared hope. Yet, since dusk of yesterday, they had gone unwatered. Early dew, and moisture from the chewed yucca flowers, had been their only drink. Now, some instinct wild and keen breathed on the ambling beasts. It whispered of something ahead; something for which their parched tongues and throats so urgently craved.

Much later, with the whole column in full swing, Tracey wheeled about and called up Mackilvray to ride point with Mansella. The right-hand flank was covered by Starett and Fourche, while Bristow rode on the left. Tracey dropped back and began helping Garston push the drag. Occasionally, one of the flank riders put his horse round in a sharp turn, cut off a darting steer and returned it to the column.

Drag dust thinned as herd and riders drew into the storm area. Above the Sierras and almost directly ahead, the sun hung like an orange disc, its warmth diminishing before evening's cool approach.

A band of antelope bounded across a draw and vanished as suddenly as they had appeared. The speed of their movements was a more than violent contrast to the labouring herd. It held a warning significance, and Tracey sent his mount from the drag at a quick run. The whole column had perceptibly slowed its place. He saw the darkness of pain in their red, dust-caked eyes, and it showed in the lolling tongues and drooping heads. His glance moved away, narrowing on the westering sun, and abruptly he stood in the stirrups, calling, 'Faster, boys! Faster!'

He neck-reined the pony in a tight caracole and raced past Bristow and signalled George Mansella back. He turned again, slackening speed, making sure that the two punchers far over to the right understood.

He swung back into the drag, shouting hoarsely, 'We gotta push 'em harder, Zing...!' and Garston nodded and lifted his deep, sing-song voice above the rumbling din. The cry was taken up; riders shuttled back and forth on lathered mounts, urging the jaded beef herd to a quicker gait.

The sun dipped and vanished behind the mountain peaks in a riotous blaze of colour; the sky splashed with hues, swift-changing and brilliant.

From way ahead, Mackilvray's shout sailed thinly back, and Rebel sent his buckskin around in a last demanding effort. Not far beyond lay the last, low ridge before the misty line which was Ute Creek, and along the strengthening breeze the scent of water drifted to nostrils choked and dry.

Mackilvray had swung well clear in anticipation, but Rebel's warning shout was instinctive and he saw the two far riders veer quickly. And on this flank, Mansella and Bristow were just as watchful, pulling out wide as the herd broke and surged forward to the creek with a new-found strength.

From the Long Rail camp, Pinto sent four riders to take over from Tracey and the others. A half-hour later, with darkness descending, the herd had once again become a slow-moving solid shape, easy to handle and bed down for the night.

By nine o'clock supper was finished and most of the weary punchers were fast asleep. Blackmer and Haycock were night-hawking over to the herd, and Steinhaus sat in the chuck-wagon's shadows, a rifle across his knees.

For the first time Rebel found sleep and anxiety were no bed-fellows. He cursed softly, rolled up a quirly and lit it. He climbed to his feet and stepped across to the fire where Pinto squatted, cross-legged like an Indian. Fireglow revealed the long, almost bitter lines of the man's face, the lantern jaw, brown and stubbled, the thin press of lips tightened by the knocks of a hard life. When he shoved back the battered stetson, hair showed brown with patches of white. Pinto. He had never known any other name. Rebel knew little of his past, but a man's past was not important. What mattered was his ability, his loyalty, his toughness. All these qualities the *segundo* possessed to the full, had amply demonstrated them over the years he had

110

worked with Long Rail.

He looked up and a sly grin slid over his face and vanished. 'Looks like they's two of us with a guilty conscience! But now yo're here, Tracey, mebbe you oughta know we lost a hoss.'

'In the stampede?'

Pinto shook his head. 'Reckon she took one, saddle an' all...'

'You sure?'

'Couldn't swear to it in a court, mebbe. But me an' the boys spent some time lookin' round while you was bringin' back the beef. What you gonna do, Tracey?'

'You mean about Esther Masterton?'

Rebel had been asking himself the same question all evening. Bartlett's herd was his main concern, but that alone was not sufficient to absolve him of all responsibility towards an unprotected white woman – anyone for that matter wandering alone in this dangerous country.

'What d'you think, Pinto?'

'We might run her to earth, an' string her up fer hoss-stealin'! Why'd she do et, anyway, less'n she was crazy?'

Tracey shook his head. 'I'm not sure, 'ceptin' she likely had some pretty raw deals an' figgered we was little better than Dodge an' his gunmen.' He drew on the quirly, threw the butt into the fire.

'There's a new settlement on the Cimarron

River,' he went on. 'In the Maxwell Grant territory. I told her about it. Mebbe she's headed that way…'

'You wanta find out, I reckon?'

'This place, Willow Creek. It's not so far off our trail. We kin keep the herd movin' an' ride over…' His glance levelled on the oldster's face. 'You seen what Injuns an' road-agents do to solitary travellers, small caravans. You saw the freighters' camp…'

'Yeah. I guess yo're right, but I reckon it's like drinkin' alkali water when yo're dyin' of thirst!'

'Meanin' Esther Masterton is poison? Well, maybe. But I guess we got to do what we can. How's that shoulder?'

'Good enough. Mansella dressed it again before turnin' in. Said it was healin' fine. We can push on tomorrow, Tracey, far as I'm concerned.'

'All right. But yo're doin' no chores at all, till George says okay. An' you better get some sleep.'

'I kin sleep in the saddle.'

Rebel got to his feet. 'So can I,' he said, and restrapped his gun-belt, adding, 'Who's with the herd – Rede an' Haycock?'

Pinto nodded and Tracey said, 'I'll ride around some. Don't let anyone shoot me!' He moved across the silent camp and came to the chuck wagon. He saw the dark shape of Steinhaus and called, 'I'm ridin' around a bit, Toke. You all right?'

'Sure.'

Rebel stepped to the liveoak where his buckskin was tethered. One of his spurs caught, half tripping him. He bent down and came up with the book of poems, and straightway shoved it in his brush jacket, trying to keep his mind from the girl.

He swung into leather, rode over to the herd and found Rede Blackmer. They could hear Haycock singing gently to the cattle, a cowboy song in a minor key.

'We'll push on tomorrow, Rede.'

'Straight fer Stage City?'

'What else?' Trace's sharp glance came at Blackmer's shadowy face.

'Don't you wanta look fer the girl? That's what else!'

Rebel nodded. 'She's caused trouble, but–'

'All wimmen cause trouble,' Blackmer growled. 'Leastways the wild an' purty ones do. But, how do we know where to look?'

'We don't. Except try a new settlement called Willow Creek, on the Cimarron. She may be there or Fort Maya, mebbe. Jest a slim chance.'

'If you say so.' Rede began circling the herd and Rebel reined around, keening the wind for no other reason than it satisfied his senses, filling his whole being with its wild fragrance. It was not the wind alone, but the whole sentient breathing land, and he felt it again as he had done earlier today on the way to the herd. He listened to the weird cry of a coyote, some way off, and the beauty of this star-filled night stirred him with its intangible mystery. He rode back and the spell was gone and he was thinking again of Esther Masterton.

Yet, when Tracey crawled into his blankets this time he was asleep in an instant.

7

IN THE WILDERNESS

The sun had climbed high. Its warm rays brushed her face and arms and Esther Masterton stirred, sleepily at first, and then to swift wakefulness.

All around her was the brushy, grass-filled bowl which she dimly recollected from the first pale light of dawn. Yet a deep-down instinct sounded its warning toll, and fearfully she raised up and almost cried out in terror. A man leaned against a boulder rock some ten yards or so away, regarding her in scowling interest. Her whole body tensed, as though she would spring up and leap away. And then the utter futility of escape seemed to be inexorably borne home to her and she sat back, muscles slowly loosening as she returned the fearsome-looking stranger's unwinking stare.

Grizzled hair hung down almost to his shoulders beneath the coonskin cap, and his leathery face was tracked and cross-tracked with a thousand lines and wrinkles. He wore a fringed and greasy buckskin shirt and leggings of the same material, darkened by dirt and weather. A black carbine lay at his feet and a long pistol showed from the belt at his waist.

He removed the short-stemmed pipe from his mouth and spoke in a rusty kind of voice. 'So yuh finally woke up, missy, huh?'

Despite all outward sighs, there was something faintly reassuring about this man. He reminded Esther of Sam Lawler.

'Who – who are you?'

He grinned. 'Might ask yuh the same thing and what yuh're doin' hyar, alone in this wilderness! Howdsumever, the name's Dick Taylor. Got a shack mebbe a coupla miles from hyar.'

'How – how–?'

'How did I find yuh? Wal, jest stumbled across some tracks an' follered 'em. Ain't many folks pass this way an' then not on their lonesome.' He studied her a moment or two, puffing at the fragrant-smelling pipe. 'Looks t'me like yuh could use some hot victuals–' He stooped, picked up the carbine and stepped towards her, and she drew back, at once afraid. And then he smiled again and the clear blue eyes twinkled with amusement. 'I ain't intendin' yuh any harm, but it shore looks like you're needin' a mite o' help, lady.'

She nodded slowly and reached her swift decision – the only one she could really make if she were to survive and find the way to Corral Flats along the Arkansas.

'My name's Esther Masterton. I was travelling with a small freighter outfit to Santa Fé. We was ambushed by Charlie Dodge an' his outlaws. They kilt everyone, 'ceptin'–'

Taylor's eyes widened. 'Dadblast it! I jest heard o' that fracas from Uncle Dick Wootten an' the Military. Say! No wonder yuh look plumb scairt...'

He hunkered down beside her and with an awkward gentleness tentatively stroked her head, as though comforting an injured animal. She found herself recounting parts of her story, even including her escape from the Texan's camp.

Presently he straightened up, and she watched him stride over to the still grazing pony and lead it back. For a moment Esther hesitated, then she stepped into leather and Taylor caught the reins and led the way through a series of tangled game tracks descending the while until reaching a broad stretch of grassy, tree-fringed land on which stood a rough shack built of unpeeled logs. A nearby creek murmured softly in the drowsy afternoon...

She sat back in a home-made chair of timber and bull-hide, watching through half-closed eyes as the trapper fed wood to the stove and set pans of vegetables and meat to heat. When they came to eat, Esther found the food tasted as good as it smelled, and

117

after awhile she leaned back and her glance touched him almost boldly. 'I'm thankin' you, Mr Taylor. I reckon you jest about saved my life…'

He grinned, highly pleased, and pointed to the dirty dishes. 'Yuh wanta repay me, then mebbe yuh'd clean up this mess.'

It was poor enough repayment, she reflected, unless… But she closed her mind to the thought and set about her task willingly, half-gladly.

She carried the plates and dishes to the sandy creek and cleaned them. When she returned to the shack there was no sign of the old frontiersman, and for a while she felt a kind of relief…

She must have slept, for suddenly she became aware that the room was much darker and Dick Taylor was standing at the door, a hindquarter of deer slung across his shoulder.

In the half-light Esther felt his eyes on her. He heeled the door shut and hung the meat on a pot hook jutting from the hut's ridgepole.

Hurriedly, Esther caught up a twig from the wood box and thrust it into the dying stove. When the kindling had caught she moved across and lit the lamp; she adjusted the wick, listening to the soft movements of Taylor as he shuffled behind her in moccasined feet.

Suddenly she whirled about, her body pressed back against the cupboard. The trapper was perhaps four-five feet away, staring at her, and his gaze travelled slowly up and down. She could not be certain whether his words brought relief or not.

He said, 'Reckon 'twas them Texicans as rigged yuh'all out like a man, huh?'

She could only nod her head, thinking, *Why did I ever come here? Why didn't I fight like I fought Dodge's savages and Long Rail?*

Abruptly Taylor turned, knocked the dottle from his pipe, and sprawled in the chair which the girl had just vacated.

He said dry and easy, 'Git the idea outa yuhr head, Esty. I told yuh fust off, yuh ain't gonna be harmed...'

'Mebbe some folks wouldn't call et harmin' a woman,' she whispered in a thick voice.

'Yuh're right there, Esty,' he grumbled. 'Nor would et with some. Now yuh – wall I got yuh figgered different. Reckon thar'll only ever be one nigger in yuhr life...'

'Nigger?'

'Shucks! Jest the way we old fool mount'n men talk. Easy now, kitten. I'm gettin' past sech foolish pranks. Reckon et won't be many years I got left, an' huntin' an' trappin's nigh done for. Like them other niggers, Bridger an' Wootton an' Fitzpatrick an' all the rest, time's runnin' out fast...' He grinned. 'Not that yuh ain't got as purty a figger as I ever

119

seen, 'specially in thet shirt an' pants...'

Esther's face and neck flamed and anger struggled with shame and fear. Yet, when she found the courage to return his gaze, she saw that he was looking past her, into the distance. No! Not into the distance, for there, as a rule, lay the future. Old Dick Taylor was gazing back into the past, and the zest of full living sparkled in his blue eyes; it lay channelled deep in every line and crease of the saddle-leather face.

'I tumbled Injun girls from the time I was a man,' he told her with astonishing frankness. 'From the Missouri Forks to Santa Fé. But' – he leaned forward in the chair, and momentarily his being, if not his mind, returned from the old trails of the past – 'life warn't jest sparkin' up to a comely Shoshone or Arapaho maiden, en' mebbe some of us'll be remembered fer other things! Sure, we was called squaw-men! But never renegades, thank God! An' we blazed a few trails here an' there, Esty, an' helped make things a leetle easier fer emigrants an' sech travellers...'

She took a deep breath, expelled it slowly, and in her green eyes lay a faint, misty wonder.

She said in a low voice, 'Then you – you don't want...'

The trapper got to his feet and padded across and looked down at her, limned there in the chrome lamplight. 'Esty,' he growled. 'I'm gettin' on fer seventy, darn near as I kin figger.' He cackled, but she was no longer afraid, nor did the rusty laughter of this old frontiersman have power to chill her as before. For once, Esther Masterton had gazed into a man's eyes without seeing mirrored there the images of Kitty, of Ma, and the evil men who had destroyed them.

His head nodded, vaguely directional, towards the single burlap-covered window frame. 'Soon mebbe, I'll be jinin' the Mimbreño an' Mescals along the Upper Gila. A few more years…' He shrugged and Esther saw all these thoughts march across his rugged face. 'Uncle Dick,' she said softly, 'will you show me the trail to take to git back to the Arkansaw Valley?'

His gaze stayed on her a long moment, while he tamped fresh tobacco into the briar and lit it. 'Sure I will. But yuh ain't told me much, hev yuh? F'r instance, why was yuh so all-fired eager to quit thet Texican camp an' throw yuhrself on the mercy o' this wilderness? Plumb lucky yuh bin, Esty, not t've run into a party o' war-painted bucks. Yuh was safe, I'd figger, with a cow outfit. How come?'

When she did not reply he touched her arm lightly.

He said, 'Yuh don't haveta tell me anythin', but … I shore like yuh callin' me

121

Uncle Dick.'

It was a strange scene here in this isolated single-roomed shack. The girl seated on a stool near the stove; the oldster listening to her tragic story and beginning now to understand the motives underlying her irrational behaviour...

He knocked ash from the pipe, squinted across at her in the lamplight, nodding slowly. 'So yuh ain't aimin' to haid fer the Cimarron settlements. Yuh're fixin t'git back to this place, Corral Flats, along the Arkansaw...'

'Sure. Like I said, Uncle Dick. We stopped over there, one night on the journey out. Oh, it's not much of a place, but at least I've got a friend there; this girl Isobel Payte...'

'Wal, supposin' the Texicans come lookin' fer yuh? Mebbe this Rebel hombre yuh mentioned'll likely go ridin' to Willer Creek or even Fort Maya...'

'You figger I'm obligated to Long Rail?' She paused and went on in a lower voice, 'Guess I must seem pretty ungrateful, but et's not like that! If I'd a'known– But, well, what's the use in tryin' to paddle back upstream? An' I still wouldn't be sure o' some of them Long Rail men! Oh, maybe Tracey Rebel was – kinda different – like you, Uncle Dick. But–'

'Sure. Yuh had only jest bin taken by Dodge's murderin' helions; yuhr friends along with Uncle Tobe, kilt… What else was yuh to figger?' He rose from the chair, soft-footed across to the door and stood a moment listening. Then he unbarred the door, looked out into the night, careful as always not to silhouette himself against the light behind.

'Reckon 'tis about ten o'clock, Esty, an' time we was turnin' in.' He closed the door and crossed back to the stove.

He said slowly, 'I guess yuh ain't obligated to make fer Willer Creek or Fort Maya, way I figger it, kitten. Sure, I'll see yuh on the way to Corral Flats. I already cared fer yuhr hoss along with mine. Tomorry, we'll make a right early start.' He picked up a saddle blanket from the rough-hewn bunk in the corner and moved back to the door.

'Wh-where you goin', Uncle Dick?'

He grinned again. 'Reckon et ain't proper fer me to be sleepin' hyar tonight. Thar's a shed around the back which Ole Man Taylor is pleased to call a stable…'

She sprang from the stool, moving swiftly, and caught hold of him by his arms. 'D-don't leave me, I…'

He stared down at her, surprised by the vehemence in her voice, by the expression in her eyes. And all at once she laid her face against the soiled buckskin shirt and wept, and some of the bitter gall flowed out from her. Later, when she raised tear-stained eyes, the old man saw them as twin pools of green water, clearer now for the rain that had flowed from them.

For all his years, he picked her up and laid her like a child on the cot, covering her warmly with a fur robe.

'Thank you, Uncle Dick,' Esther whispered, and held up her face to be kissed. Quickly, Taylor wiped his mouth and whiskers and implanted a soft, chaste kiss on her cheek. Her eyelids lowered and her body relaxed in the instinctive knowledge of security.

He waited until she was deeply asleep, then he wrapped the blanket and several plews around him and lay on the earth floor by the barred door, the Henri rifle held in his gnarled hands...

Three days later they were almost a hundred miles from the shack in New Mexico territory, and but for 'Uncle' Dick Taylor, Esther would have been long dead...

On the morning of the fourth day, Taylor kicked out the fire and waited for the bucks to show themselves. He knew they were there because he had smelled them, likewise had the sorrel. He turned to the girl. 'How's the loads in that Colt's gun, kitten?'

She checked the pistol he had given her, ejected two spent shells and reloaded with fresh ammunition. Her face was pale, but

124

beyond that she evinced little sign of apprehension. Esther Masterton was fast learning, with Dick Taylor's help, how to survive in this hostile country.

She said quietly, 'Okay, Uncle Dick. Like you said the other day, I don't do any shootin' less'n you tell me. They – those Injuns down there – they ain't what you'd call friendly?'

He shrugged and scowled down towards the dozen or so warriors who had half-circled the small rocky camp. 'Mebbe they are; mebbe not. Don't look like they's painted up; likely a small huntin party or mebbe jest scoutin'.'

'But they're not Mimbreño or Mescals?'

'Naw! They's Comanches. They know we's hyar, but they ain't certain sure how many–' The trapper broke off and, rifle in hand, climbed to his feet.

Four bows lifted, already fitted with arrows, and three breech-loaders gleamed in bronzed hands. The leader made a quick restraining gesture, wondering perhaps if this were a trap, or if this long-haired hunter were a decoy of some kind.

'Stay put, Esty, an' keep me covered all the way,' Taylor growled, and unseen by the Indians thrust the carbeen into her hands, taking the Navy Colt's gun in exchange and ramming it into his belt.

'*Uncle Dick! Don't–*'

125

But Taylor was already walking towards them. He moved slow and easy and held a smile on his face, and presently gave the peace sign and addressed the leader in slow Spanish. A flutter of uneasiness stirred him as he went closer. He stopped, allowing them full time to get used to him, as he would have done stalking any wild game. These Comanches were probably amongst the fiercest of any of the tribes, and Dick Taylor had met up with them many times in his life; more than once he had narrowly escaped death at their hands. But since the incident with Peta Nocona, their chief, the old frontiersman had remained more or less immune. Rash indeed would be the brave to flaunt the wishes of the great Peta Nocona, but, Taylor reflected, there was always a chance some brash buck might shoot first and ask questions after.

As soon as he had greeted them, he drawled the magic name Nocona, and as he had fervently hoped, it was sufficient for these warriors to lower their weapons and listen to the white hunter's talk. Now they began to realize that this was *Tay-law*, the man who had rendered some service to their chief, and his pale-face wife.

'We have meat,' the trapper told them. 'Yuh-all are welcome to eat with *Tay-law* and his white squaw.'

Their dark gazes flickered up to the rocks

126

and brush. They saw only the black muzzle of a gun and a glimpse of corn-silk hair, and wondered what manner of squaw this man had taken for himself.

Finally their leader spoke haltingly. 'We would eat with the white hunter and his squaw. The white man is our enemy; but *Tay-law,* he friend of Chief Peta Nocona.'

The old man nodded. And now, casually and without trepidation, he swung around and led the way back to the camp two-three hundred yards away. He called out to the girl, 'Put up yuhr gun, Esty. They's eatin' with us.'

He wasn't at all sure whether she had the nerve to obey him without question. But she paused only momentarily, eyeing the Comanches warily, yet somehow calmed by their aloof attitude. For each one accorded her no more than a single penetrating glance before tethering his pony and squatting cross-legged on the ground.

Quickly, Esther saw to the fire, setting a sulphur match to fresh brush, much to the studied interest of the eight near-naked Indians. Taylor busied himself spitting a shoulder of venison, turning it slowly over the crackling flames.

An hour later, their paunches full, the Comanches rose to their feet. The leader grunted the one word *'Gracias'* and in a moment they were astride their ponies and thundering away south-eastward.

She had been scared all right. But she was learning to cover her fears, even as she had covered herself with the buckskin jacket Taylor had given her. Now she loosened the rawhide strings and turned to him.

She said softly, 'How did you manage it, Uncle Dick? These Comanches are – well, I usta hear Mr Wishart an' Mr Lawler talk about them…' She spread her hands in a faint gesture and between her dark brows a single line appeared. 'You mebbe lived with them, sometime, Uncle Dick?'

He remained hunkered down, packing together their few items of equipment, and shortly he looked up at her, a lop-sided and half-bitter kind of smile hoisting his mouth.

'Ain't so simple as that, I reckon, Esty. An' mebbe et's somethin' I wouldn't do agin– Hell! I dunno! 'Twas only that she implored me not to…'

'She?'

He laid aside the gear and reached for his pipe. His leathery face was long with memories as he gazed into the slowly dying fire.

He said presently, 'Yuh ever heerd o' Cynthia Ann Parker, kitten?'

'Why, that name does sound kinda familiar, but – no, I cain't…'

'I'll tell ye then,' the trapper grunted, 'an' I mind it like it was only yesterday, though it must be more'n twen'y years.' Taylor re-

128

moved his pipe and spat into the fire, before resuming. 'East of Waco, down in Texas, is Fort Parker. They was besieged down there, way back around '36, I guess it was. Oh, sure, plen'y forts an' settlements has bin attacked by Injuns since then, over the years. But this was somethin' special, 'cos a big party o' Comanches an' Kiowas attacked an' captured a girl, Esty, mebbe not even as old as yuh! A young buck, name o' Peta Nocona, took her, for he was leader of the Comanche war party.'

'And the girl was – Cynthia Ann Parker!'

'Right! Strangest thing that ever did happen, though, was when I stumbled across Nocona's camp mebbe a year, mebbe two years afterwards. I'd bin follerin' tracks fer days, figgerin' ef'n the Injuns was friendly I might trade a leetle with them.'

'But all the time they were really Peta Nocona and his band?'

The trapper nodded. 'I didn't know they was Comanches fer sure, an' I was set to risk my scalp, anyways, on account I'd gotten 'bout a thousand bucks' worth of furs cached away.' He shrugged. 'I'll never know how it happened, I guess, but all of a sudden I was face to face with an Injun squaw astride a paint. Leastways I figgered she was Injun – at first. Then I saw that fer all her sun-burned face an' hands, she was white, an', here's the funny thing, Esty, for straightaway I got the feelin' she was Cynthia Parker…'

'But weren't you rushed and overwhelmed by the camp, Uncle Dick?'

Taylor chuckled. 'Guess et ain't once in a blue moon yuh ketch a big Injun village nappin', but so fer they hadn't smelt me out, the camp bein' in a hollow 'bout a mile away!'

'An' this young girl, Cynthia – and she – was she already the chief's…?'

'Sure. But right then I figgered she'd be wantin' to escape. 'Twasn't till later I learned sech details.

'I'd got a tight hold on the pony's hacka-more, an' I said, "'Missy, I reckon yuh're Cynthia Ann Parker, ain't yuh, as was captured by Peta Nocona at Fort Parker?"'

The oldster gazed at his pipe speculatively as though somewhere in the smoking bowl lay the answer to the whole puzzle.

He went on, 'She shore fit me like a wildcat at fust! Teeth, nails, feet an' then she got to implorin' me not to take her back…'

Esther's lovely eyes widened in shocked surprise. Yet her face was alight with the fascination of the story. She said, 'Yo're not tellin' me, Uncle Dick, she absolutely *wanted* to remain with those – those savages?'

Taylor nodded and jabbed the stem of his pipe in the girl's direction. 'She did, fer sure! An' don't believe thet jest on account they fit the white man, Injuns is allus savage, Esty!'

'But – what did you do? Jest leave her be?'

The trapper ruminated awhile. 'I guess I coulda got her away, at thet. I'd heerd the Military an' the Rangers was still lookin' fer her. But – wal, I dunno, Esty. The crazy thing was she seemed so all-fired *happy*, dressed up like an' Injun in deerskins an' dyed porcupine quills. I guess she was at that. This Nocona musta treated her well enough, married her – she wasn't no slave nor brow-beaten hostage, an' that fer sure!'

'What happened?'

Again the oldster chuckled. 'That time I came as near losin' my h'ar as ever was, fer Nocona himself an' three-four braves suddenly jumped me! Seems like the chief had come out lookin' fer his squaw ... was kinda worried...'

'Then it was this Cynthia as saved yore hide?'

His eyes lifted in mild surprise to her face. 'Seems even kittens knows the answers afore the questions is put. Sure, she prattled away in a kinda Border Spanish an' a few Comanche words, tellin' Nocona he'd gotta spare my life now an' at all times in the future! Yep! She told that warrior-husband of hers I could've taken her back 'stead of which I'd listened to her pleas – how she wan'ed to remain with the greatest of the plains tribes an' walk with the greatest leader the Comanches had–'

131

'She really *believed* this, Uncle Dick – I mean about the greatest tribe...?'

The grizzled frontiersman scratched his head in thought. He said, 'I guesso, Esty. Reckon she wasn't bein' held against her will.'

'And – after all these years – she is still with them – still the wife of Peta Nocona?'

He nodded. 'Cain't be any doubt, else those bucks would 'a tried liftin' our h'ar. 'Twas when I gave the peace sign an' spoke the chief's name an' told 'em who I was. From then on, like yuh saw, they acted plumb peacable...'

8

ROSINA McCALL

The Long Rail column moved steadily northward, with Pinto acting as Trail Boss.

Towards sundown of the second day, when the riders began swinging the herd from the trail, Rebel and Blackmer rode up lathered with the sweat and dust of hard riding. Later, after supper, Mansella stacked fresh buffalo chips on to the fire and looked across at the two men and laid his one question at Tracey Rebel's feet.

Rebel shook his head. 'We found Willow Creek all right. We even saw Maxwell himself...'

Pinto said, 'Heerd tell he's got more'n a hun'ed peons workin' for him.'

'That's no lie, I'd say.' Rebel paused, rolled and lit a *cigarrillo*. 'Sure is a big man with big ideas, too. He's buildin', farmin' an' raisin' stock. Figgers to spread out as well, clear through to Vigil an'–'

'Bigawd, Tracey, though! D'jou ever see such a hombre fer drinkin' an' gamblin'?'

'Rede's right, boys. Lucien B. Maxwell don't believe in doin' anythin' small. He drinks, gambles, rides like a Comanche and spends *dinero* like water. Yet all the time he's buildin' an' doin' a fine business with the army posts...' Rebel drew on his quirly, looked at the faces around him in the fire-light. 'He's had no news of any solitary travellers, least of all a woman, but he said to look in at other settlements on the way north.'

Steinhaus said, 'Then that's all—'

'No, et ain't all, Toke.' Blackmer's voice rumbled across and tipped the finality from his saddle-partner's words. 'Me an' Tracey shore done some ridin' these past two days an' we ain't figgerin' on quittin' yet.'

Pinto said, with a sly look, 'Fort Maya, huh?'

'We got to do what we can,' the Long Rail ramrod grunted. 'A girl alone, orphaned an' friendless, captured by bandits, then rescued by wild Texicans!' The faintest smile moved his wide lips and stirred for a moment in the depths of his eyes. 'Sure! You hombres ever figgered what we musta looked like to her? Not much better'n Dodge.'

'But—' Pinto said, and stopped, and Blackmer growled, 'Tracey's right. Fourteen men as wild as them fifteen hun'ed head of shaggy beasts we's drivin'! Leastways that's the way et looks, don't et? Tomorry, we're gonna kill a coupla ponies gettin' to Fort Maya. After that...'

'After that?' Zing Garston repeated quietly.

Rebel got to his feet. He threw the stub of his cigarette into the flames and gazed out into the starry darkness.

He said softly, 'Nothin' to stop us keepin' our eyes open and askin' questions while we push on. But me an' Rede 'll be with the herd from then on out. We gotta push that beef hard for Stage City.'

Soon, except for the night guards, they turned in. And so soon again it was dawn and once more the grinding day's drive began. A tin-plate of preceding days, except for those times when danger had attacked in the shape of hostiles, storms, stampedes. Rebel thought as he turned and spurred after Blackmer. 'But there's fifteen – no, fourteen – of us to face all that! My God! How can one lone girl ever hope to survive…?'

Blackmer was a fine man to have riding along. His philosophy was simple and devoid of any conflicts. He knew only a loyalty to Texas and Long Rail, and whatever those two mistresses demanded, he was prepared to give without question or reserve. He would have been shocked even by the thought that this should not be so.

He waited on the nub of a low hill overlooking the army post, wishing, amongst other things, that in place of a canteen of lukewarm water he had a bottle of rye. The thought led him on to their destination – Stage City; the *dinero* Tracey would be able to pay them out, once the beef was sold, *if it were sold,* whetted his appetite for the wine, women and gambling that would be theirs for a few days.

Across the yucca-splashed, tawny grassland, the gates of Fort Maya opened and Blackmer saw Rebel emerge. He knew at once that Tracey had met with no success. It was there to see, in the way he rode the buckskin, easily as ever, but almost, Rede thought, with disinterest. He put his own mount to the down grade and pulled in alongside Tracey some ten minutes later. The big black-bearded Texan scowled across towards the post, as though the blame, if any, lay there.

He said gruffly, 'No luck, Tracey?'

Rebel shook his head. 'Nary a sign of anyone travellin' alone. An' they's bin quite a few Injun bands rovin' lately. Maya's had its hands full sendin' out scouts an' details, keepin' a sharp look-out.'

'Utes?'

'Not only them, Rede. Comanches an' Kiowas. Not big war parties, but small rovin' bands. Huntin' mostly, I guess, but that don't mean they's any more friendly.'

'You figger…?'

'How the hell do I know, Rede? Mebbe she's already a squaw in some *jacal*. Mebbe even a slave bein' beaten an' worked like a bayeaux nigger!'

Blackmer spat, rolled a quirly and passed across the makings. When he held a sulphur match to Rebel's *cigarrillo*, their glances met and locked for the space of a second.

'You considered what else, Tracey?'

Rebel looked away. That was something he could not believe. He could not *feel* it; therefore, how could it be true? Yet – death was no respecter of persons, and women died on the frontier as well as men. The possibility that Esther Masterton no longer lived, had to be faced, whatever.

Blackmer said, 'Me an' Pinto can git them longhorned bustards to Stage City, Tracey, if you wanna stick around this neck o' the woods!'

Tobacco smoke stung the foreman's eyes and he wiped sweat and grime away with the red *rebozo* around his throat. And then he grinned and laid his glance on Blackmer's swart face, and said softly, 'What makes you say that? Angeline, mebbe?'

'Mebbe. Well, what you figger on doin'?'

'Push on, like we told the boys last night! We're dam' near into Colorado now. 'Sides which, we're totin' around nearly thirty thousand of Bartlett's dollars!'

'Why, sure, Tracey. I wasn't–'

'I know. Let's ride, you ole sidewinder.'

They spurred away, heading for the trail

137

herd, as the lowering sun tinged the western peaks blood-red.

Slowly the Long Rail beef herd moved ever forward, skirting the sprouting settlements of Vigil, Stonewall, Torres, Cuarto, Primero, Segundo. At each one Rebel stubbornly continued his enquiries concerning Esther Masterton, and each time he returned to the waiting Blackmer he shook his head. 'Trail's dead as mutton.'

'Come to that, Tracey, never was any trail, thanks to that Noo Mexico storm!'

The punchers were in no doubt that their trail boss still thought and hoped with regard to a golden-haired wildcat. But mostly they shrugged, not talking about it unless, as sometimes happened, Tracey referred to that particular eventful night.

The going remained rough. Vast areas of land were still almost unoccupied save for a few isolated and hardy settlers' homesteads. Large herds of buffalo were frequently seen in the blue distances, and in their wake Indians and buffalo hunters trailed the great shaggy beasts. And, as before, the snaking brown column of steers did not go by unremarked by the red men. Only that the herd, flanked by its hard-eyed riders, was a truly awe-inspiring sight, did smaller bands of Arapahoes and Comanches refrain from attack as they roved far northwards.

Sometimes they gave the Texicans a wide berth altogether, yet at other times they drew up atop some nearby hill, deliberately skylining themselves, watching with glittering eyes and brandishing bows and rifles in defiant, threatening gestures.

'Reckon they shore as hell hate our guts,' Steinhaus remarked one day as the herd swung steadily towards its destination. 'Spoilin' fer a fight thet bunch, Tracey. Look at 'em! D'you ever see critturs so eager to kill?'

Tracey observed the band of twelve–fourteen Indians little more than silhouettes and too far away to identify the tribe. But near enough for Long Rail to note their resentful demeanour.

'Guess you cain't blame 'em, though, Toke. Mountain men, trappers, freighters, the army – all pushin' westward into their hunting grounds! Now they's watchin' Texan cattle an' riders on the move, likely for the first time, an' they see us as jest another threat to drive them further westward and kill their herds.'

'But we ain't kilt no more'n one-two o' them bufflers!' Pinto had ridden up and now voiced his mild objection.

'How do *they* know how many buffalo bones lie bleached on the trail behind us, Pinto? Try tellin' them we's only fixin' to kill a few, jest enough to help out our meat, an' that we're only travellin' through this country.'

'Yeah.' Steinhaus nodded thoughtfully. 'Guess we ain't the only ones, is the trouble. Lookit thet bunch o' hunters four–five miles beyond them rocks ahaid!'

The small Indian band had also seen the hunting party and if their thoughts had been turned towards attacking the trail-herd, they were now seemingly diverted towards this latest threat.

Much later, when Indians and buffalo hunters had long since passed out of sight, shots were heard echoing faintly from the north-west. The firing continued intermittently until it faded completely. Only the steady rumbling of cloven hooves and the occasional wild yippees of riders as they kept the column in line, disturbed the quiet; and day followed day and trail town drew steadily nearer...

'Five-six miles is all,' Rebel told them early one morning. 'Me an' Rede's ridin' in ahaid. Pinto! Keep the beef movin' slow an' easy while we run this Vic Shafto to earth.'

Towards late afternoon the two trail-stained riders gigged their mounts into the new settlement, making the nearest livery and barber shop their first ports of call. In back of Weekes' barber shop, Rebel and Blackmer indulged in their first hot baths in over two months. Both men had bought new shirts and kerchiefs as well as fresh underwear. Now, refreshed and fully rigged, they struck Main Street again. Blackmer surveyed the shacks and frame buildings and spat expressively. 'Ragtown, huh!'

Tracey nodded towards the saloon opposite, on whose false frame front were painted the words, 'The Golden Fleece Saloon.' He smiled. 'Quite a place there, Rede. Looks like it's bin built to last. Let's get fleeced to the tune of a coupla drinks before we find Shafto.'

Blackmer grinned through the freshly trimmed beard. 'That shore is the bestest idea you had since them baths, Tracey boy. 'Sides which, we might even find our buyer right here inside. Kinda make things easier, I reckon.'

They stepped through the dust and loose garbage on the street and tromped across the plank walk.

'We seen some plush saloons back in Houston, Austin an' San Antone,' Tracey said when they pushed through the batwings. 'But even in Texas they don't come much better than this.'

'Bigawd!' Rede smacked his lips. 'You kin say that seven times over!'

It was a vast and ornately decorated room. A long bar stood to one side, behind which a small army of Aprons dispensed beer and whisky to dry-throated traders, freighters, hunters, Army men on furlough, and a host of characters not so easily definable. At the far end was a stage lit with naphtha flares, and over to the other side were tables for monte, roulette and faro. Even with the booths there was still room enough for fifty-sixty couples to pack the dance floor section, though at this early evening hour the customers were mainly occupied with their drinks.

Rebel planked a gold eagle on the counter, called for a bottle of the best rye, and asked the barkeep, 'Would you know the whereabouts of Vic Shafto?'

'Texicans, huh?' the man said, glancing from one to the other. 'An' all spruced up—'

Blackmer's huge hand came out and gripped the shirt-sleeved arm like a vice. 'See hyar, mister—'

But Rebel grinned. 'Easy, Rede,' he said, and turned to the barkeep. 'You were sayin' about Vic Shafto—?'

A voice interrupted Tracey, a low, vibrant voice, and even above the reek of sweat and dirt and kerosene he caught the faint perfume as he turned and looked at the woman who stood now at his side. She said quickly, 'What's the trouble, Henry?' and her gaze traversed from Rebel's sun-blackened face to the Apron's quick-shifting eyes.

'No trouble at all, Miss McCall, I guess. I was jest joshin' with these Texicans, is all.

142

And – and, this gent was askin' fer Vic Shafto...'

'Really? Mebbe I can help.' Her eyes lifted again to Rebel's face and on to Blackmer. Like Henry, she recognized them for what they were. Drovers. Sure enough they were not U.S. Marshals.

'Mebbe I can help you cowboys,' she repeated, 'if you'll step into my office for a moment...'

Tracey smiled. He said in Spanish, *'Gracias, señorita,* we will be honoured,' and saw the quick warmth flare for a moment in her dark eyes. Then she turned, leading the way to a door at the end of the bar.

Blackmer caught up the bottle and shot glasses and followed on into the office. With the door closed, much of the outside noise receded.

She sat in a ladder-backed chair at a roll-topped desk and indicated comfortable chairs for the two men. Tracey removed his hat and looked across at Rede, and the big bearded man followed suit before placing the drinks atop an oval table.

'Why – how did you know I would understand the lingo *señor?*'

Tracey sat regarding her a moment, wondering how such a lovely creature came to be running a honky-tonk saloon in this new, raw settlement. Her hair was piled high in the Eastern fashion and shone under the kerosene lamps like burnished jet. Her eyes, shaded by the thick lashes, were a dark blue. But the olive skin and high cheekbones more than hinted at her Spanish ancestry.

'Ah, but of course' she smiled. 'You would have seen many Spanish and Mexican peoples, down in Texas – too many, mebbe,' she added quickly and gestured in a typically Latin manner towards the table. 'Please pour your drinks, gentlemen, and allow me to introduce myself – Rosina McCall – proprietor of the biggest and cleanest gambling joint west of St Louis!'

'That's quite a claim, Miss McCall, but I shore am inclined to believe it!'

'I'll beat the hombre as says different.' Blackmer growled and poured rye into the two glasses and raised his thick brows questioningly.

She shook her head, her eyes warm again. 'If you don't mind...'

Rebel said, 'This is Rede Blackmer, Miss McCall, an' I'm Tracey Rebel. We represent John Bartlett's Long Rail an' to prove it we done drove nigh on fifteen hundred head o' longhorns clear from the Neuces to–'

'You've really brought fifteen hundred cattle, *on the hoof,* all this way? Why, I – I guess I didn't think such a thing was possible. I guess I didn't believe Vic–'

'So you know him, *señorita?*'

She arose from the chair and crossed over

144

to a cabinet against the papered wall and poured a small glass of red wine. 'A woman's privilege, isn't it, Mr Rebel?'

'To drink *tequila,* or change her mind?' He watched the deeply red lips soften and then firm again as her thoughts returned to the practical. She came back to the chair; the swish of her taffeta dress, the verbena scent, and the alabaster smoothness of her bare shoulders and arms were food and drink to these starving trail men.

She was used to the heat of men's gaze and she knew well enough the desires that stirred beneath the calm surfaces of the Texans. Yet, as she returned their level gazes she saw an honesty of purpose and, above all, a chivalry. Once these men had crossed the town's dividing line, no woman there would be immune, because she was there for one purpose alone. But here, even in such a place as the Golden Fleece, a woman would be as safe with such men as though she were in church.

All these things Rosina felt and saw within the space of those first few moments. And by the time she was reseated she had determined upon her course of action.

She said in a low voice, 'Yes, I knew Vic Shafto very well. Too well. He told me he had plans, big plans for buying Texas cattle, selling them to nearby army posts. He had even planned to build a single-track railroad, complete with spur line, loading chutes and all the rest, so he could ship more beef direct to eastern markets.'

'Sounds like he's quite a business man, Miss McCall,' Rebel murmured. 'Takes vision, I reckon, to think up schemes like that, an' with scarce any railroads west of Kansas.' He paused a moment before adding, 'You said you *knew* him, ma'am. You – you ain't suggestin' he's kinda vamoosed someplace?'

'You might call it that, Mr Rebel. Vic Shafto was found shot dead in an alley right by here, about three weeks back!'

'Dead!' Somehow Tracey had never contemplated such a thing happening, even though he had visualized the possibility of Shafto ducking out of the deal for some reason or another.

'Bigawd!' Blackmer's tone was shocked. 'Don't tell us we trailed them longhorns a thousand miles fer nuthin?'

'But – shorely they's someone else; other cattle buyers, Miss McCall, who'd take our herd…?'

'Oh, sure.' Her full lips stirred in a faint smile. 'And what do you suppose you'd get, once they knew you was stuck with a herd that size? Make no mistake, Mr Rebel. News gets around fast. It wouldn't be long before every two-bit operator – even the army posts themselves, mebbe – was offerin'

146

you two-three dollars a haid–'

'But ain't there a demand fer beef?' Black-mer said.

Rosina nodded. 'Yes, but you've gotta have the right contacts and have a system lined up, like Shafto did, for getting the beef to market at the lowest cost in men, time and money!'

'So Shafto wasn't operatin' for a company or eastern syndicate; he was workin' this idea single-handed?'

'More or less.' She drank the remainder of the wine and set down the empty glass, staring thoughtfully before her. She said slowly, 'You've come a long ways, you Texans, and you musta bin to some trouble and danger, trailing a big herd through Indian country. Mebbe … I could buy your cattle and at a fair price. Does that surprise you? Well, before Vic died – I mean the last time I saw him alive – he was tellin' me of his plans for the future, what he was aimin' to do and a few of the contacts he'd made–'

'Then you know–?'

'I know a little – not much. Enough to put you in touch with at least one–two other men, though I reckon your profits'd scarce be worth countin'.'

'Meaning that they'd beat us down, but that they'd give you a square deal?'

She saw the sudden mistrust in Tracey Rebel's eyes. She got up and crossed to an

147

inner door and called, 'Race! I want you.'

In a moment a man showed up in the doorway, slight and wiry and with iron-grey hair and saddle-leather skin. Rosina closed the door. 'This is Jed Race,' she told the Long Rail punchers. 'My right-hand man. Jed! Meet Mr Rebel and Mr Blackmer. The *señores* 've hazed over a thousand head of beef clear through from Texas. What would you say they'd fetch?'

Race pushed back the low-crowned hat and scratched his head. He stared at the two men and then transferred his gaze to the ceiling.

'With Shafto daid, Miz Rosina, I'd say they ain't got much chanct.' He brought his gaze down from the ceiling and pinned it on Rebel. 'Y'see, mister. They's still plen'y buffler meat around. Hunters is goin' out most every week an' though it's hides they're after, they still tote in meat – even if it does mean the Injuns goin' short–'

'The price?' Rebel said.

Jed Race shrugged. 'Mebbe you could 'a fixed et somewheres around twen'y, twen'y-five bucks a haid, with Shafto. Now, I dunno as you'd git much more'n what the hides an' hooves'd fetch.'

'A few dollars each?' Rede growled.

'Yep.'

'All right, Jed.' Rosina laid her quick glance on Race. He turned and withdrew

148

into the back room and carefully closed the door. She looked across at Tracey. 'You don't believe me, do you...?'

'Aw! Miss McCall...' Blackmer's deep voice rumbled out in hurt protest, and Rebel stood up suddenly and reached for his hat. He looked at this beautiful woman who, despite the contrast, reminded him so strongly of Esther Masterton.

She moved over and stood before him and her sober gaze lifted to his face.

She said softly, 'It'd dam' near clean me out of cash, but I'll give you twenty bucks a haid an' take your word the critturs are in good shape. That's – well, somewhere around thirty thousand dollars.'

'Say!' Rede grinned, 'ef that ain't mighty fair of you–'

'Why would you do that, Miss McCall, less'n you could sell again at a profit?' Tracey's gaze bored into her.

'I – I don't quite know how to make you understand or believe me.' Her voice was low like the rustling breeze on a summer evening. 'I guess it's because I feel responsible...'

'*Responsible? For our cattle?*'

She had turned away again, and now, quick and impulsive, she whirled and sent her glance hard at Blackmer as though sensing his unspoken support.

'Responsible,' she answered carefully, 'for

the fact that you have no buyer! Oh, don't imagine that The Golden Fleece is a philanthropic institution...' Her eyes chilled and Tracey read something there in her face, something he had not seen before. He let his hat fall on to the sofa and rolled up a quirly and waited.

'You see, gentlemen,' Rosina McCall whispered. '*I* killed Vic Shafto, right here in this room, three weeks back; an' only Jed Race an' me knew about it. Now, like a fool, I've told a couple of complete strangers who cain't even take my word–'

'Forgive us, *señorita*. Mebbe we – mebbe I didn't trust you fust off. Likely enough Rede here's got more sense in thet thick skull of his than I gave him credit fer. But–'

'Spare me the necessity of going into all the details,' she interrupted. 'It was just that Shifto began taking – liberties. He figgered he could–'

'Why, the dirty–' Blackmer struck the palm of his hand with a balled fist. The sound carried like the crack of a bull-whip. 'You ain't suggestin', Miss McCall, he – he harmed you in any way...?'

She smiled and shook her head. 'It was to stop him – harming me, I shot him. After – Jed carried the body outside and dumped it...'

'But no frontier jury would convict a woman under these circumstances...?'

150

'No, Mr Rebel, probably not. But it would likely have meant the end of me here in town. I – I wouldn't 've bin allowed to carry on, mebbe. Preacher Farrer has tried to close this place down more than once. He – he's called me a sinner and harlot... I guess he really is religious in a queer kinda way.' She stopped suddenly and again her eyes hardened. 'I have ten percentage girls working for me here, *señores,* and I – well I try to be like a *duenna* to them. Believe me, Mr Rebel, when I tell you they are all–'

'Hell!' Blackmer swore. 'That ain't religion, callin' you names like thet, Miss Rosina!'

Tracey sent his gaze quickly around the room. He said quietly, 'You mean, apart from losin' all this – everythin' yo've worked fer – these girls of yours 'd have no place to go...?'

'No place this side of the line! Which means they'd either starve or end up in the downtown sporting houses.'

Rebel stepped forward and proffered his hand and, half-doubtfully at first, Rosina returned the handclasp. He said, 'You jest bought yoreself nearly fifteen hun'ed haid of Texas cattle, Miss McCall. But there's one condition...'

'A catch, eh?'

He shook his head and smiled. 'Now it's *you* as don't trust *us*. No! It's jest that I'm sellin' you the herd fer twen'y-five thousand dollars...!'

9

CORRAL FLATS

They sat their ponies atop a low ridge and Dick Taylor pointed ahead across the rolling prairie. 'Yuhr troubles is over now, Esty, I reckon. Cain't be much more'n half a day's ride 'cordin' to what yuh said. Corral Flats is likely the next settlement along B'ar Creek.'

Her eyes followed the direction of his snarled and sun-brown hand, and she saw the low line of bright green foliage bordering the shallow creek.

'Sure. I reckon this is mebbe a little north of the route we took outa Kansas. Now, if I head south-east away–'

'Yuh got et, Esty. Foller the creek. Say! Yuh sure yuh don't want me to see yuh clear through...?'

'No, thanks, Uncle Dick. Already you done more'n enough.' Impulsively she reached forward and laid her hand over his. 'I'll make Corral Flats by afternoon, easy, an' once there all I gotta do is look up Isobel Payte.'

Taylor nodded at the gun butt protruding from the waistband of her denims, visible now with the brush jacket loosened. 'Yuh made good use o' thet old cannon onct twice since we lit out. Reckon yuh best keep it.' He handed her a leathern pouch of ammunition and lifted the reins of his horse in readiness to turn. She leaned dangerously from the saddle and caught his weatherbeaten face between her hands and laid warm lips to his cheek.

She drew away and spoke in a low, thick voice. 'Thank you for all you done, Uncle Dick. Mebbe – one o' these days I'll see you again…'

She waited not a moment longer, but reined south-eastwards and kicked the paint into a fast trot. Once she turned her head and through blurred eyes saw him pointing the sorrel steadily south. She waved a hand, but Dick Taylor's eyes were on the trail. For a mountain man there should be no pro-tracted farewells…

Through the shimmering heat of late afternoon Esther saw the scattering of wooden buildings which was Corral Flats. It seemed years back since she had stopped over for that brief visit with Isobel, when the wagon-train had camped nearby for the night. Searching her memory, she realized it could have been no more than a matter of five or six weeks. Yet, somehow, the place seemed changed. Perhaps it was that the buildings now looked more hopeless, even more tawdry and insubstantial than they had done before in the softening starlit darkness.

She made an effort to throw off the faint forebodings that assailed her, and squared her shoulders and rode straight and tall in the saddle like a man, and swirled up the dust on Front Street as she slid the pinto close in to a hitching rack.

Most always there was a good reason why a town suddenly mushroomed on the sage-covered plains or in a valley. Even the settlements further westward towards the Rockies grew and flourished because men had ventured in search of wealth. Gold, silver, copper; minerals well worth scrabbling from the bowels of the earth or panning from the streams. There were cow towns too, where stores and trading posts and saloons all contributed their lively and essential requirements for the existence of outlying ranches. Sometimes a town was born overnight because some sly landshark had bought lots and promised a railroad. Once every so often communities were premature and died stillborn.

Maybe, Esther thought as she climbed from the saddle, this was the trouble with Corral Flats. For the moment she was too occupied to observe the glances thrown at her by this small town: bold and meaningful from the loafing men on the street, shocked, hostile looks from the sun-bonneted women. And from the doorway of the *Bugle* offices Isobel Payte gazed downstreet, her china-doll eyes widening slowly in bewilderment as the tall, range-rigged figure straightened up from the cinches and turned and mounted the plank-walk. For a brief moment Isobel had thought it might be some young rider from the plains – even a messenger from brother Virgil – but a second glance was sufficient to dispel any doubts as to the newcomer's sex.

Isobel felt her cheeks redden as she gazed in wonderment at the girl's brazen garb: the over-tight denims encasing shapely legs, the open brush-jacket and woollen shirt, and the corn-gold hair piled high beneath the battered stetson.

'Landsakes!' Isobel exclaimed suddenly. 'Esther!' and ran forward heedlessly and clasped the girl in her arms and laughed and winced at the same time as the Navy Colt's butt pressed into her body.

'Isobel! I shore am glad to see you... I ...'

'Esty! You – you – oh, I don't know quite what to say! I never thought to see you again. There are so many questions I have to ask! Why for goodness' sake are you dressed like – like...'

'All in good time. Maybe we can go some-place where we can talk...?'

'But of course.' Isobel glanced quickly around, aware now of the stir they were causing, and hastily she caught her friend's arm and led her into the newspaper office, straight through past the printing room and up a short flight of stairs to the parlour.

'Sit down, dear, over there on the sofa,' she smiled. 'You look dusty an' tired. Put your shoes – er – boots... Oh! Just rest yourself, honey, while I fix you some coffee. Then you must tell me–'

Isobel Payte's blue eyes rounded in sheer astonishment as she realised that Esther had stretched herself full-length on the sofa and was already fast asleep...

Much later the two girls sat in the lamplit kitchen. Little by little, Isobel squeezed Esther's story from her, all the while listening with a kind of shocked fascination.

'But, Esty! How could you possibly survive such ordeals? How could you come through alive? That storm and those terrible men...!' She paused for a breathless moment. 'Did they...?'

Esther smiled. With the complete recounting of her recent experiences, much of the horror had receded. Now she regarded her friend with faint amusement.

'Y'know, Isobel, you really are more bloodthirsty than I had you figgered! I shore believe you'd like me to say that Uncle Dick Taylor was young an' handsome an' virile, an' swept me into his cabin; an' that there was no alternative...'

'Oh, no, Esty! You – you misunderstand me!' Isobel's blue, innocent eyes looked pained for a moment. She moved across the room and lit another lamp and started to set the table for supper.

'It – it wasn't that at all, dear, and besides which,' she added, unconsciously betraying herself, 'it was the Texan – the man Tracey – I was thinkin' about…'

Esther Masterton's hand moved in a sweeping gesture. 'Please Isobel…' She began to smooth the dress with which her friend had furnished her. 'How – how is the newspaper goin'?'

'Fine! Jest fine an' dandy, Miss Masterton!' The two women swung towards the now open door. Isobel smiled. 'Why, Virgil! How come you're back so soon? I didn't expect you for another day at least! Say, you remember me tellin' you–'

'Sure. I remember, Belle!' Virgil Payte's wide smile made the heavy face more handsome. 'I even remembered the name as well as the description.' He removed the dust-covered stetson, stepped into the room and closed the door.

'You – you must have a – a very good memory, Mr Payte.' Esther's words tumbled from her lips despite her efforts to remain calm, even aloof, before this flashing blade who was Isobel's brother.

'Sure was a pity I missed out seein' you last

time, Esther,' he said softly. 'An' back in Kansas, when you two were friends, I was away east learning how to become a newspaper man. 'But' – he turned to his sister – 'I hope mebbe *you* can persuade Miss Masterton that Corral Flats has got a future an' likewise has the *Bugle!*'

'Well, Virge, at least Esther'll be stopping over a while and I won't hear different. For that matter, I guess I'd like her to stay on indefinitely.'

'But, Isobel! I – I–'

Virgil Payte threw his hat onto a chair. 'What about some chow, Belle? We can talk about Esther's problems after we–'

'But, Mr Payte–'

'Call me Virgil,' the newspaper owner smiled, and placed three chairs at the partially set table. It was an enjoyable meal and warmly pleasant to hear Isobel chattering away and slyly interspersing her talk with snippets from Esther's recent experiences. Over coffee the golden-haired girl smiled at her friend. She said, 'Well now, Isobel, since you've told Virgil a little, mebbe you had better tell him the rest. I guess,' she added soberly, 'I owe it to you folks to let you know everythin' that's happened.'

'I began to smell a story some while back,' Payte grinned, 'an' I reckon this one's goin' to rate banner headlines.'

'You mean – you wanta *print* it?'

For a moment Esther stared aghast into Virgil's handsomely florid face, and Isobel said, 'Sure. Why not, honey? Virge won't print anything *too* personal; nothin' you would not want folks to know. Why, Esty, it – it's a wonderful idea and–'

'And I've just had a wonderful idea too!' Payte's dark face glowed with enthusiasm as he glanced from one to other of the girls and leaned his arms forward on the table. But it was Esther on whom his bright gaze mostly rested. 'We need more help with the paper,' he said. 'It's growin' fast, like the town itself, whatever strangers may figger. I guess you could get around some an' pick up pieces of news an' gossip – pull in a few ads, mebbe earn yourself some *dinero*...'

'But I couldn't do anythin' like that! Besides, I–'

Virgil Payte glanced shrewdly at his sister's dress which Esther Masterton wore. He said easily, 'Guess you'd like to feel independent, wouldn't you, Esther; be able to buy yourself clothes an' bonnets an' such gee-gaws? 'Sides which, you'd find it interestin' work, meetin' folk, buildin' a place for yourself in the community!'

'He's right, Esty.' Isobel rose and poured fresh coffee into the cups. 'Virge is a mighty busy man these days, ridin' far and wide in search of news. We'd be working together, you an' me, right here in town– Oh, there's so much to do you've no idea...'

'You – you help as well, Isobel?'

'Sure she does.' Payte grinned. 'Drumming up business, chasin' clients for their money, reportin' on gossip an' social activities. Like Belle says, I got my hands real full gettin' news from outlying places. Why, I'm fixin' to ride over to Stage City soon as next week's edition is on the streets. They say it's a hell roarin' settlement – plen'y goin' on there to interest the folks even in Corral Flats.'

'How far is this place?' Esther heard herself asking the question and wondered vaguely why she had done so. Off-hand, the name conveyed nothing to her, except...

'Stage City? Less than fifty miles an' jest about inside the county line.' He smiled before adding, 'At least you must stay here an' help Belle till I get back. Tomorrow you can meet Lije Farley – my compositor.'

'Lije not only sets up all the type,' Isobel explained, 'he operates the printing press and most always I'm around to fold the papers. What do you say, Esty?'

'It's – why I guess it's real kind of you both to give me the chance. I – I'll shore try an' make a reputation–'

'You already done that!' Virgil laughed. 'The whole town's humming with talk about the yellow-haired girl who rode in dressed like a man...'

Esther Masterton bit her lip. 'That's some-

160

thing I gotta live down, I guess. And mebbe,' she added softly, 'this is the way to do it…'

It seemed scarcely possible that she had been in Corral Flats two weeks; that Virgil Payte had gone to Stage City and was due back any day. Esther was honest enough to acknowledge that she missed him; but the hours were so crowded, thanks to Isobel and the paper, that she had little time in which to brood or think.

There was always shopping or household chores to be done and fitted around sewing-bees, small social gatherings and the inevitable drumming up of advertising space for the *Bugle*. And in this, as well as in the matter of collecting payments, Esther Masterton was remarkably successful.

'You mean you've actually sold old Fred Kearley on the idea of taking a series of three column ads, Esty?' The fact that Isobel herself had consistently failed to induce the town's hardware merchant to book more space did not dampen her admiration for Esther's success.

'He – well, I guess he's not such an ogre, Belle,' Esther smiled. 'In fact he's really rather nice, though I cain't say the same of Mrs Kearley. An' that reminds me. I shore am dreading that tea party Mrs Springett's givin' next Saturday. Have I *really* gotta go?'

'Look,' Isobel told her friend. 'You're

doing fine. In less than two weeks folks are forgettin' how – how you looked when you first hit Coral Flats.'

'I didn't have much idea myself what I looked like. No comb or brushes, no mirrors 'cept the rivers an' creeks; out in the wilderness – I reckon I was jest thankful to be alive, is all.'

'Sure, Esty. And don't think the town isn't beginnin' to realize what a tough and raw deal you had. Another thing,' Isobel continued quietly, 'Virgil's quite a leadin' citizen – well respected – his friendship's somethin' worth having, I guess.'

Esther Masterton rose and crossed the room, laying an arm lightly around the dark-haired girl's shoulders. 'Don't you know how grateful I am to you, Belle – you an' Virge both? Mebbe I was a fool not t' have left the caravan that night an' stayed on here! Then I'd never have met up with those – those *animals*...' Her sage-green eyes glittered at memory of Dodge and his outlaws, and Isobel said briskly, 'Come on, Esty. We have to hand this copy into Lije so he can set it up ready for Virge to okay soon as he gets back.'

They descended to the big press room adjoining the office and on the same instant hoof-beats pounded out along the street and stopped abruptly outside.

'Maybe that's Virge now!' Isobel ran through into the office and Virgin Payte

162

stepped through the open door. He was covered in dust and weary, but the light of enthusiasm shone brightly in his eyes and he sent his quick, probing glance at Isobel and on to Esther, beyond. He grinned at them and cuffed his hat back on his curly black hair. He said, 'Have I got news that'll stand this town on its ears...?'

'Mebbe you have,' Isobel rejoined, 'but come inside an' tell us, else folks won't have need to buy next week's issue!'

In the upstairs kitchen, Virge Payte sprawled back in a chair and poured hot coffee down his throat. 'All right, girls. I won't keep you on tenterhooks any longer. This is it! That cattle outfit you told us of, Esty, Long Rail from Texas, has driven its herd clear to Stage City! Not only that,' Payte grinned, wiping his moustache, 'but darn me if they haven't *sold* the herd! D'you get that? Sold over a thousand beef on the hoof and which has bin trailed nigh on a thousand miles! Sold it in a place that's not even a shipping point...'

'You mean...'

'Look, Belle...' Virge leaned forward in his chair, face sober now through the impact of this recently acquired news. 'First off, let me tell you this is history in the making! Do you realize that no sizeable herd of beef has ever been hazed up from Texas, through Injun country? I tell you, this is something big –

163

banner headlines – mebbe even a special edition.'

Isobel said quickly, 'I'm beginning to follow you, Virge. This *is* important! Yet, as you say, Stage City's not a shipping point; there's no railroad, no spur line or loading pens–'

'I'm coming to that, Belle, and I've got the whole story!' He turned his gaze onto Esther. 'Mebbe you don't realize what a stir you caused with those Texas cowboys, honey. D'you know that they're *still* lookin' for you?'

'You didn't tell them…?'

Payte shook his head. 'What do you take me for, Esty. You told us enough when we ran your story to put Belle an' me in no doubt–'

'I want no part of them,' she whispered fiercely. 'Long Rail! Tracey Rebel! Dodge! What's the difference? Keep them away from me, Virge! D'you understand?'

He moved across the room and touched her lightly, reassuringly. 'You don't figure I'd lead them here, do you?' He gazed at her warmly a moment before turning to his sister. He said, 'In any case, Long Rail wasn't figurin' on staying in Stage City over long. A week at the most as I heard it. Then they're hitting the trail back to Texas with enough *dinero*–'

Behind Isobel Payte's innocent, doll-like face worked a brain that possessed no little of the shrewdness that was Virgil's. She sat frowning thoughtfully, looking from Esther to her brother. She said, 'I still don't understand, Virge... Who would have bought such a large herd of beef, unless they... Maybe someone there had some way of disposing of it fast; else they would surely stand to lose out on the deal!'

Payte grinned approvingly. 'Sometimes you're real smart, Belle. Like you say, a herd that size has got to be disposed of *muy pronto*. Only two alternatives in a territory with few or no railroads. One: the buyer sells to the nearest army post, and for that he must have had terms of contract already drawn up and agreed to by the army. Two: the buyer doesn't sell the beef at all, but keeps them as a ready-made herd with the idea of going in for cattle raising on a large scale! And,' he finished, slapping his hand on the table, 'that's just about what's happened.'

'So mebbe someone in Stage City is fixin' to raise cattle?' Esther said. 'What's odd about that?'

Payte smiled. He was always smiling, it seemed like. He looked at Isobel. 'You remember that day last month when I took you into Stage City an' showed you around?'

'Sure. But–'

'You remember that saloon across from the Lewis House?'

'Or course, Virge. How could I forget? It's called the Golden Fleece, and the reason I remember so well is on account you pointed out Rosina McCall to me – the woman who runs the place. Landsakes, Virge! That woman is so beautiful I hate her!'

Payte's booming laughter rattled the cups on their shelf-hooks. 'That's a dam' good reason for hating anyone, honey, if ever I heard one! Sure, she is a handsome lookin' filly even if she does rule that joint with a rod of iron.' He paused and stroked his moustache and brought his thoughts back quickly. 'Well now, *she's* the buyer of those Texas longhorns an' *she's* the one fixin' to go in for stock-raising, and what d'you two pretty girls think of that?'

'I still think your story angle should only be concerned with Esty and her escape from the Long Rail camp,' Isobel declared. 'What difference does it make to the readers who the buyer is?'

'You should know better'n that, Belle,' Virgil admonished his sister. 'Men out-number women about fifty or a hundred to one along this part of the frontier an' they are the ones who buy – *and* the ones who like to read all about a woman like Rosina McCall...'

'Is – is she really so – so lovely?' Esther's voice was so low that for a moment the newspaper owner was scarcely aware that

166

she had spoken.

Now, with something of a triumphant flourish he drew an envelope from his coat pocket and carefully unwrapped the contents. The girls saw a small copper plate on which appeared to be photographed the head and shoulders of a woman. Virgil handed it to them. He said, 'The copper plate is a daguerreotype, as you may have guessed.'

Esther Masterton looked at the plate. Despite some blurring in places it was clear enough for them to see that the sitter was indeed a lovely girl, and Esther's gaze lifted to Virgil's face and in her green eyes there lay the smokiness of a low-smouldering fire. She said softly, 'This is Rosina McCall?'

'Sure is, and I'm gettin' Lije to copy it.'

'You're going to have Lije make a woodcut,' Isobel exclaimed, 'just like the ones he does for the ads?'

'You got it, Belle. Sure-fire front page stuff, eh?'

Mrs Springett's tea parties were one of the high lights in the life of Corral Flats. On the shaded porch, tables were set out and here the chosen few gathered and chattered. Occasionally the talk was general, impersonal; more often one of the ladies injected the toxic words: 'Now you mustn't tell a soul about this, but I did hear that Mrs White…'

Mrs Springett believed strongly in the caste

system. It spoke much therefore, for Esther Masterton's personality and her achievements with the newspaper, that Mayor Springett's wife should have so quickly accepted the newcomer. The Springett home was probably the best in town, and the 'back yard' more of a well laid out garden. Here, under the sharply watchful eyes of Flora Springett, the children were allowed to play.

Esther Masterton sat at the end of the porch, watching the afternoon shimmer of heat along the horizon, and her eyes turned towards the north-west and she thought: 'Not so far beyond those low hills lies Stage City!'

Elsa Green, the dressmaker, spoke in a light voice, yet one which she took good care would reach Esther's ears. 'Mr Payte certainly knows how to get *news*. Did you see yesterday's *Bugle?*'

Mrs Kearley, hard-faced and forthright, said. 'Of course. Reckon everyone in Corral Flats read about those Texas killers an' how Miss Masterton out-smarted them!'

Marion Furndyke, whose father was the town assayer, murmured, 'Seems to me, Miss Masterton was protected by Providence. If–'

'May I have some more tea, Mrs Springett?' Isobel Payte asked sweetly.

'But of course. You, too, Miss Masterton?' Esther smiled and nodded. 'Please don't get up.' She took her cup and saucer to where Mrs Springett wielded a large silver teapot. She turned her eyes on the others there, and in particular, Marion Furndyke.

Esther tried hard to modify her strong Kansas accent. She said, 'What about that picture Virgil printed? Don't you think this Miss McCall shore is pretty?'

Flora Springett snorted. 'Pretty! Well, maybe if you like–'

'Saloon girls?' Marion Furndyke smiled. 'Ah, now, if that Texan–' She stopped suddenly, colour rising to her cheeks, and Isobel said clearly, 'If which Texan, Marion…?'

'I was going to say that likely, he'd be the kind of man who'd consider this saloon woman beautiful, though not sufficiently attractive to marry, I'll wager.'

Esther let go with one sharp word: 'Why?'

Mrs Springett, surprised at the tone, raised her eyebrows, and Miss Furndyke said, 'That's the kind of men these Texans are, aren't they, Miss Masterton? You said so yourself in that *Bugle* article!'

Esther didn't answer. She was suddenly overwhelmed at the resentment she felt towards this sour-faced young girl.

Mrs Kearley said acidly. 'Why do you suppose those cowboys elected to put up at a saloon, 'stead of the Lewis House? That's right, isn't it, Isobel?'

Isobel Payte's smile was a little frosty.

'Virge certainly said that the foreman and one-two others were staying at the Golden Fleece. But–'

Esther banged her cup down and expelled a rasping breath of exasperation. 'What does it matter to any of *us* what they do or where they stay? They got a right to lead their own lives, haven't they?' She paused a moment, only to control the sharp rise and fall of her breasts. Never anything but blunt, Esther put her deep feelings into a final devastating remark. 'Mebbe they're doin' jest what yore husbands an' brothers do, when they ride to some raw town on "business"!' She turned sharply and moved away. Behind her, the shocked silence lay like a yawning gap over which Esther Masterton knew she could never now retrace her steps...

10

NEWS OF ESTHER

'What's bitin' you, Rede? Any reason why we shouldn't pull out tomorrow an' head back to Texas?'

They were seated upstairs in Rosina's private parlour. The girl herself leaned back on a sofa set against the wall. She looked from the big, bearded Blackmer across to the Long Rail boss and spoke softly:

'Rede has done me the honour of asking me to become his wife, Tracey. Does that come as a surprise to you?'

Rebel stared, and Rosina saw the hardness in his eyes. She said, 'This girl, Esther Masterton. Mebbe she gave you a raw deal, Tracey. I guess she did. Does that mean you're against *all* women? Does it mean that you figure I don't love Rede an' wouldn't make him a good wife?'

He laid his glance on Blackmer and spread his hands in a small gesture of indecision and he heard Rede say gruffly 'Look, Tracey boy. I ain't fixin' to duck out on you or Long Rail. I'll ride back with you-all, jest like we agreed.'

'What you aimin' to do here?'

'Cattle,' Rosina said, and arose from the sofa and crossed over to the table. 'In case you're wonderin', Tracey, Rede an' me – he – we only fixed this last night…'

'He's free, white an' twen'y-one,' Rebel said.

Rosina leaned forward, laid her smooth hand on the foreman's arm. 'You figger yo're losin' a friend, as well as a top-rider! Well, maybe you are in a way. But that's not the whole thing–' She stopped and her soft glance turned on the man she was going to marry. 'You tell him, Rede.'

'Sure, honey.' He leaned across the table. 'Rosina ain't figgerin' on sellin' all the herd, Tracey. She – that is, we – figger on doin' a little ranchin' on our own account. They's grazing land fer miles around an' that ain't all. We reckon to start up where Vic Shafto left off. Sure, he was a lousy sonafabitch all right, but reckon he had some smart ideas, like tradin' with these army posts an' plannin' a single track line, east from hyar…'

Rebel nodded. A moment ago the news of Rede and Rosina had come as a shock, or so it seemed. Now he knew that for days past he had been half expecting some such thing.

Whereas most of the riders, excepting Garston and Mansella, had been having a time with liquor and cards and women, Rede Blackmer had remained unusually sober and

172

quiet. Rarely had he strayed far from the Golden Fleece, and Rebel recalled how Rede's eye had followed every movement of the lovely Rosina McCall.

Maybe it was not so strange after all. Blackmer, despite his rough upbringing and the shadows across his backtrail, was a man to ride the river with. And Rosina? Tracey knew by now she was no ordinary saloon girl. Likely, she, too, had a past of some kind. Whatever else, she was true to her word. She kept a tight rein on the girls in The Golden Fleece, and she had spoken no more than the truth when she had claimed that Preacher Farrer was trying to close what he fanatically called 'this blatant den of iniquity.' Just so long as folk like Seth Farrer caused no real disturbances or violated the peace, Broge Slattery, the town Marshal, had no call to interfere.

Tracey's glance lifted and he looked deep into the eyes of Rosina and saw the hunger and love and integrity that shone un-ashamedly there. Maybe this was what she had been waiting for, for a long while: a man like Blackmer, big and strong as an ox, yet underneath as gentle and loyal as a dog.

'I reckon,' Tracey grinned, 'I forgot to con-gratulate you both.' He threw a sly glance at Blackmer and tilted Rosina's chin and kissed her gently on the cheek. 'When's it to be, *chiquita?*'

'Whenever Rede says so.' Rosina smiled. 'We – we wanted to get married before...'

'Sure. But you don't want Pastor Farrer to...?'

'Hell, no!' Blackmer's tone was vehement. 'They's a Spanish padre at the Mission, 'bout ten miles outa town.'

They were three days out of Stage City. Hampered only by a few cow critturs for their own needs, Long Rail had travelled better than eighty miles by dusk of this evening.

Pinto moved across to Rebel, fashioned a cornhusk cigarette and passed over the makings, grinning. 'Whoever'd figgered that big ox, Rede...?'

Tracey lit the quirly and blew smoke, watching Mackilvray and Starett build up the mess fire. The camp echoed with the purposeful sounds of men accustomed to the routine of such chores.

'Sure,' he nodded. 'And wherein was the sense makin' him ride back to Nueces – him a bridegroom only two hours?'

Pinto jerked his head towards the men around the fire and chuck-wagon. 'What with whoopin' et up fer more'n a week, then celebratin' a weddin' ... why, I guess some o' them cow-wrasslers is only jest realizin' they got heads on their shoulders!'

Toke Steinhaus moved across from his

174

saddle and hunkered down in front of the two men. 'Reckon we'll miss the bustard, but I'm sure glad fer his sake. You figger, Tracey, she'll do him right?'

'Yeah,' said Rebel softly. 'I do. Mebbe jest like Angeline – mebbe more so. I–'

'Hold et!' Zing Garston called from beyond the picketed ponies. He had turned his head towards the camp and every manjack looked up in startled surprise. Garston's rifle gleamed in the early starlit night. 'Sounds like riders,' he warned, 'but mebbe only one. I can't tell yet.'

Rebel was on his feet, already spreading his men out in a circle away from the camp-fire's light. It could be just a false alarm. It could be anything. He sent Jed Starett and Bristow to join Garston near the cavvy; Fourche and Barringer crouched down in the shadows of the chuck-wagon, whilst the others lay and listened and waited.

Shortly they heard the rataplan of hooves over the rough ground. 'Zing was right,' Tracey called. 'Only one rider so far, but watch it, boys!'

The as yet unseen horseman was holding his mount to a steady gallop, though not at full stretch. It seemed evident that he was heading straight for the camp, without any attempt at subterfuge. Tracey rose up from the grass, carbeen in hand. His eyes were narrowed in the direction of the galloping

175

horse and for some strange, unaccountable reason the image of Esther Masterton flashed before his mind's eye. And then a familiar voice bellowed out of the night, raising itself far above the clatter of pounding hooves. 'Hold et, Long Rail! This is Blackmer!'

He was no more than a dark silhouette in the night, but they knew that shape all right and the dramatic way he rode, and they knew that voice. Wasn't another one like that anywhere east of Taos!

'Bigawd!' he shouted, reining his lathered mount. 'You helions shore have bin burnin' leather.'

'Looks like you bin fannin' the breeze some yoreself, Rede!' Tracey loomed out of the shadows as the Long Rail men climbed to their feet. 'What the hell is it, Rede; you need our guns?' Rebel's voice, sharp with anxiety, cut like a blade through the babble of noise.

'Naw! Guess I didn't aim to worry you, Tracey boy. Jest a leetle news I figgered you might wanta hear. News as might go stale was it kept overly long!'

'If it's nothin' serious, then to hell with it!' Rebel turned around. 'Chuck! How's about some grub for the men an' thisyer new boy?'

For a little while they camp was dangerously noisey. The banter, coarse but goodnatured, and the laughter raucous, as at any shivaree.

'Wal, ain't you gonna tell us-all what for you bin trailin' us?' Pinto asked.

'Shore I am.' Blackmer turned to Rebel, unmindful of the camp's wide-eyed interest.

'See hyar, Tracey. Here's what Rose an' me figgered you-all should know. Day after you hit the trail fer home, a girl comes ridin' into Stage City. She was plumb tuckered out an' her hoss was all lathered.' He paused and drew a deep breath. 'The pinto wore a Long Rail J.B. an' the girl...'

'...was Esther Masterton?' Rebel had half-sensed it from the first moment of Rede's arrival. But Blackmer's thick brows drew down and he said, 'How in hell did you–?'

'I didn't know. Was jest a shot in the dark, is all.'

'Did – how is she, Rede?'

'She – she's all right – now. Rosina's takin' good care of her.'

'What d'you mean – "all right *now*"? For God's sake–' Rebel stepped forward and griped Blackmer's arms with a strength that made even the giant wince.

'Easy, Tracey! Wait till you hear the hull story. Then you can jedge how lucky she's bin...'

Slowly Rebel's grip slackened and his hands fell away. He wiped the sweat from his face and in the tense following silence Pinto got up and fed fresh fuel to the fire. It was the signal for each man to carry on with his appointed chore. A huge kettle of beef stew was lifted onto the iron spit and soon the savoury smell drifted over the night breeze, watering the mouths of the hungry cowboys.

Later, Rebel got up, filled three cups with coffee, and returned to where Blackmer and Pinto squatted. Pinto gulped down his hot drink. He said, 'I'm seein' to it, we got plen'y lookouts posted, Tracey. Any special ideas?'

'No. 'Cept mebbe we oughta screen that fire some.'

The *segundo* nodded and moved away and Rebel said softly, ''Twas a risky thing to do ridin' all this way alone, Rede.'

'What are *amigos* for? 'Sides which' – Blackmer's beard parted and his teeth gleamed whitely in the night– 'Rosina figgered you oughta know *pronto*, Tracey!'

'But–'

'All right. Here's how it was, far as we made out from Esther herself. Seems like she, too, had some purty dark an' bloody shadows across her back trail – way back in Bleedin' Kansas. Then, on top of that, Dodge strikes an' murders them freighters an' captures the girl fer sport. Like you said, I guess, Esther Masterton had us figgered as *mal hombres*.'

'So she planned her escape, prepared to take her chance out there?'

Blackmer nodded. 'Bigawd, Tracey! Luck or Providence shore rode at her stirrup. She musta bin plumb lost after the storm. Likely would 'a died but fer an' old mountain man, name o' Dick Taylor. He looked out for Esther and guided her to the Arkansaw. On the way they met up with Injuns a coupla times an' drove 'em off. Next thing, Taylor saves her from a dozen or so Comanches.'

'How could he do that? Comanches have a hankerin' fer white women, 'specially ones like – like Esther.'

'Sure. Remember Cynthia Ann Parker...?'

Rebel listened in silence while Blackmer told what he knew. Some of it had been coaxed out by Rosina, but mostly Esther had volunteered the news and had answered questions without evasion.

Tracey was still gazing out into the night long after the ex-Long Rail rider had finished.

Presently he said, 'Coupla things you've not cleared up, *amigo*. Way back, you said somethin' about Esther was all right *now*. How near was she to – to cashin' in?'

''Twasn't that,' Blackmer growled. 'But – wal, I guess you got a right to know the truth. She'd come to Stage City lookin' fer *you*, Tracey. When she found Long Rail'd pulled stakes I guess she jest finally quit tryin' an–'

Rebel's voice was like the dry rustle of leaves. He said, 'Yo're not sayin' she tried to

179

kill herself?'

'Worse'n thet, in a way. I pulled her outa the Red Light District – jest in time!'

A long time later Blackmer said softly, 'What was the other thing on yore mind?'

'I bin wonderin',' Rebel answered slowly, 'jest how you knew I might want this news so bad...'

The other laid his glance on the now sleeping camp. 'They-all figured you took a shine to the girl, Tracey. Even Mackilvray, accordin' to Zing, said it was on yore face. But I guess by the time we got to Stage City, *they* figgered you'd done forgotten.'

'Meanin',' Tracey suggested with a meagre smile, 'you didn't see it thet way?'

'Yeah. I reckon. But it was really Rose–'

'Sure. Why not! Another woman! A good woman and lovely, Rede. Your wife. She'd be able to read the sign a dam' sight clearer than you or me!'

'You've got it, boy! And now what you aimin' to do, come mornin'?'

Rebel dived a hand into the pocket of his coat and produced the gold-poke which Rosina McCall had paid for the Texas longhorns. 'Twen'y-five thousand bucks less two hun'ed each for the boys – say three thousand. That still leaves twen'y-two thousand, Rede. A tidy sum an' I'm seein' it safe into J.B.'s hands personal.'

'Then you ain't ridin' back with me at

dawn? No! I guess you won't be. But thar ain't any reason why you cain't ride back *afterwards*, is there?'

'Mebbe not. I had it in mind. Meanwhile, I want you to close-herd her in Stage City; look after her, you an' Rosina both...'

'You don't haveta say any more. We'll see to that.'

'She needs someone to – to rope an' brand her, Rede, in gentle fashion. She's a wild maverick that's had a full taste of the meanness of man.'

Blackmer nodded. 'I'm ridin' out before first light. Tell the boys *adios*, Tracey. An' we'll be lookin' fer another J.B. herd before the fall. Any messages you want delivered to a certain Golden Fury?'

Rebel smiled. He replaced the gold poke and handed across the book of verse. 'Give her this, Rede, an' tell her I'll be ridin' back along this trail before September's out...'

More than a week had passed since they had quit Stage City and Long Rail was feeling the strain. Two of the six meat steers had died through being driven too fast and too hard. The ponies were gaunted down, slatsided through insufficient feed and too much riding.

Nor was it just a question of livestock, for the men themselves were jumpy, their nerves rubbed raw by the constant threats of Indians and outlaws.

In the early morning sun the Osnaburg canvas-topped Conestogas glistened along the Santa Fé Road far away to the north-eastward, and Rebel glanced at the lean, unshaven faces around him. Every drop of liquor the punchers had absorbed in Stage City had long been sweated from their rawboned bodies. Likewise, each man was cleaned out to his last *peso*.

'Men,' Rebel said abruptly. 'We need a rest, and so do them hosses. A few weeks back, some of you was honin' to visit Santa Fé...'

They looked up from their chores and the beginnings of a cautious interest flared in their red-rimmed eyes.

Toke Steinhaus said, 'You joshin', Tracey?'

'No. If you-all wanta swing west, we'll do it. 'Twil add no more'n a week at most an' we made good time thus far.'

Pinto said softly, 'You know we's all broke...?'

Rebel nodded. 'But you got the other half of that bonus comin' to you. J.B. said two hun'ed bucks apiece in the event of sellin' the herd.'

'But...'

'Sure. The rest was to be paid when we got back home.' He shrugged. 'So? J.B.'s not goin' to worry if you drink it now!'

They grinned then, and an animation

182

rippled the honed-down faces, and by the early forenoon the cavalcade was heading for the gateway to the Spanish south-west.

'Thar she is!' Pinto turned and grinned at the eager men around him. 'Santy Fé!'

Below, in the valley of the Rito de Santa Fé, lay the ancient and royal city: oldest capital within the boundaries of United States' territory. Yet, to the eyes of the Long Rail men, it seemed little more than a sprawling collection of flat-roofed, adobe houses along winding streets and roads.

'We'll make camp on the outskirts of the town,' Rebel said 'an' stay over tonight an' tomorrow. After that, it's straight fer home!'

They grinned and nodded their approval and took time out to scrub their faces and shave. They slicked down their unkempt hair and managed to find clean bandanas. One of the stage coaches from Independence had just gotten into the town, and when Long Rail arrived it seemed that the entire population was out of doors welcoming *Los Americanos*.

'*Hola muchacho!*' A group of dark-eyed *señoritas* singled out the figure of Tracey Rebel as he rode in, tall in the saddle. '*Americano muchacho!*' One really lovely, laughing Mexican girl called to him and ran to his stirrup with all the uninhibited spontaneity of a child. He smiled down at her

183

warmly and leaned low in the saddle and kissed her full red mouth, and the quick impulsive act rekindled the flame of longing in his heart. He rowelled the horse and the dusky-eyed maiden drew back to her laughing friends, her eyes clouded in angry bewilderment.

At sundown the clanging of the bell in the church was the signal for festivities to commence at La Fonda Inn. Rebel felt himself drawn along by the gay, carefree crowd. All around were Mexican girls dressed in their thin bright blouses and swirling short red skirts; and all were bedecked with heavy bracelets, earrings and necklaces. Like the dark-visaged men, the *señoritas* puffed incessantly on cornhusk cigarettes.

Mingling with the natives were a few trappers, mountain men and freighters for whom the richly colourful scene never palled.

Rebel found himself caught up in the excitement of the *fandango* as the *señoritas* stamped and clicked their high-heeled shoes and whirled around until their skirts stood out straight to reveal the shapely legs underneath. Howls of admiration greeted the wildest steps and more than one pretty Mexican girl was the cause of a savage brawl.

Yet, despite the hovel-like 'dobe houses, the incessant gambling, the cock-fighting and wild *fandangos,* it was not long before Tracey found himself feeling at home. Back in Texas were many places like this, yet somehow not so vividly colourful and tempestuous. He roamed the narrow, débris-littered streets alone, beginning to understand why this place, with its barbaric, festive atmosphere, threw such a spell over trappers and freighters and cowboys alike.

He dropped by one of the *cantinas* and drank the raw *aguardiente* sparingly, conscious the while of the heavy gold-poke he was carrying. Even now that the men had been paid their bonuses in full, there still remained over twenty thousand dollars to take back to Bartlett.

It was not yet midnight and somewhere, scattered throughout the town, the Long Rail punchers would be drinking and gambling just so long as their dinero or their luck held out. But Chuck Barringer and Will Fourche were guarding the wagon and livestock and Tracey decided to get back *pronto*. If they wanted, the two men could still make a night of it. Otherwise they would have tomorrow, and after that there would be no more funnin' this side of the Nueces.

With this sudden resolve he swung away from the gay, lantern-lit Fonda Inn with its noise of laughter and revelry, its strong, conflicting scents and its bright variations of colour and light and deep shadow.

He strode through the throng and past the Golden Cockerel *cantina,* and paused a moment at the end of the 'dobe building to roll a *cigarrillo*. He stuck the quirly in his mouth, wondering how many of the men would be back at the camp by dawn, nursing thick heads. He wiped the sulphur match against the 'dobe wall, shielding the flame with cupped hands, and from the alley's blue-black depths there sounded the staccatoed click of Spanish heels, the soft rustle of skirts.

She was standing there in the shadows, beautiful, provocative, this same dark-eyed *señorita* who had greeted him when Long Rail had first ridden in.

The yellow *camisa* lay bare the satin smoothness of her skin as she stepped towards him. And as though suddenly aware of the chill breeze she swept the black lace shawl around her shoulders and smiled up into his sombre eyes. She said, in faultless Spanish, 'The *Señor Americano* looks lonely. My home is nearby. Perhaps the *señor* would care to eat and drink wine with Carlotta Grenados and her brother, Ramón?'

Months of grind and sweat and fighting on the trail had worn Rebel's restraint thin. He was a man, with a man's strong impulses and desires, and Carlotta Grenados, sensing this quickly, caught her breath and wondered almost fearfully, why she had at first so deliberately played the *coquette*.

'Carlotta.' He repeated the name softly, and

186

in the half-darkness was aware only of her closeness and the perfume drifting from her shining black hair and the deep red of her parted lips. And in that off-guard moment the image of Esther Masterton faded like a ghost in the night, and Rebel held the Mexican girl in his arms and she took his kiss and gave it back without reserve.

She drew away at last, breathless, her dark eyes alight, and for a moment they stood apart and were completely oblivious of the roistering throng of revellers passing by no more than a few yards away.

He saw then the sudden strike of fear in her eyes as her gaze probed beyond, into the unlit alley. He heard the softly furtive step and half-whirled and dropped a hand to his gun. But he was too late to avoid the crashing blow that descended on his head and sent him staggering forwards. As though in a nightmare dream he heard a woman's sharp scream. Another vicious blow came at him, and with it, darkness black and impenetrable descended as he crumpled to the ground…

Rebel's first awareness was of a terrible throbbing in his head. There seemed to be a light before his eyes, bright and powerful as the mid-day sun. He struggled to achieve a sitting position, instinctively moving slowly so as not to increase the hammering pain.

He felt the pressure of strong yet gentle hands around his shoulders. Almost, it seemed as though he were lying on a bed and that someone had placed pillows at his back and head. 'Mebbe I'm delirious or plain nut-crazy,' he thought, and forced himself to open his eyes against the blinding glare. Very slowly the brilliance softened and receded, and after a while he saw that he was in a room lit only by tapers and an oil lamp. The blurred images before his eyes sharpened into clear shapes. A Mexican stood at the foot of the bed regarding him in sober thoughtfulness. Voices sounded in his ears, low and speaking in Spanish, and painfully Rebel turned his head and surprise cleared some of the pain and heaviness from him as he gazed into the lustrous eyes of Carlotta Grenados. At once the girl reached into a basin on a side table and withdrew a cold water compress which she now applied to the Texan's head.

'*You!*' he whispered weakly, and sank his head back onto the pillows…

Many of the oblong-shaped 'dobe houses in Santa Fé were little better than mud-hovels, with tiny mica windows let into the five-foot-thick walls. But this room was well furnished and spacious and the barred windows fitted with glass. Strings of peppers and gourds hung from the walls and gaily-coloured blankets added their brightness to the atmosphere of warmth and friendliness which seemed to pervade the entire establishment.

Carlotta said softly, 'First you will eat, *Señor* Rebel. Then we will tell you what happened.' Vaguely he wondered how it was that she knew his name. He had no recollection of having told her. Then he saw his shell-belt and gun hanging over the back of a Spanish leather chair, and the Mex, intercepting his glance, grinned suddenly. He said in Spanish, '*Si!* Your name is engraved on the butt of your pistol, *Señor* Rebel. That is how we knew your name. My sister–'

'She – she really is yore sister?'

'But of course, *señor*...'

'Then – then you must be – Ramón?'

The slim young man nodded and smiled. 'It is coming back to you, *si?* Maybe you remember–'

The door opened to admit Carlotta bearing a laden tray which she placed on the table beside the bed. She cast her brother a quick, reproving glance. 'Let the *señor* eat and drink first, Ramón.'

If at first he had not felt hungry, Tracey very soon changed his mind as he began wolfing the highly spiced Mex cooking. He made short work of the soup and a *puchero*, a kind of beef stew with vegetables and garnished with sauce made from minced onions, parsley, garlic and dried peppers.

He was halfway through a dish of *tortillas* when he held still as a though struck rigid. Suddenly he dived a hand into the inside of his buckskin jacket and his eyes hardened like blue-grey stones.

11

A TRUMPET SOUNDS

'The gold-poke, *Señor* Tracey, is over on the cabinet,' Carlotta said. 'The *dinero* has not been touched since–'

'Mebbe you an' yore brother'd tell me now, Carlotta,' he said quietly, 'jest exactly what happened.' He drew a long breath and added, 'Looks like I'm shore indebted to you fer savin' my skin an' the dinero likewise.'

Ramón inclined his head. 'If you will please excuse me, *señor*, I have some business to attend to. Carlotta will tell you.' He bowed slightly and with a murmured *adiós,* quit the room.

'You – you must have thought badly of me at first, *Don Rebelde...*'

He grinned. 'Spare me the undeserved mode of address, Carlotta. My friends call me Tracey.'

She smiled her understanding, telling him not without some hesitancy, how a fortune-teller only last week had prophesied that she, Carlotta Grenados, would meet a tall, dark man, perhaps an *Americano;* that this

191

would happen right here in Santa Fé, and very soon.

With characteristic impetuosity she had immediately identified the *Americano* with the old Indian woman's prophecy. After that, even though Rebel had ridden away, Carlotta had searched the town, wanting to see the Texan again – just to make sure.

'And – did you make shore,' he smiled, 'when – when I kissed you nearby that *cantina?*'

She turned away for a moment, and Rebel swung his legs from the bed and stood up, ignoring the throbbing in his head. He crossed over and caught her arms and would have kissed her, but something in the depths of those dark, shining eyes held him back.

'Don't you want to hear how Ramón came up and threw his *cuchillo*–'

'You mean he killed whoever it was figgered on robbin' me?'

She shook her head. 'Fortunately, no. In the darkness they escaped, but undoubtedly it was because of Ramón that you–'

'That I'm alive right now! I know that, Carlotta, and I cain't tell you–'

She placed soft fingers over his lips. 'You don't have to tell us anything – Tracey. We...'

He still held her arms, looking down into her lovely, olive-tinted face. 'I asked you if you made shore of somethin', Carlotta?'

He released her then, for he knew the truth, knew what she would say.

'After you had kissed me, Tracey, although I returned it, I knew, I think, that though you hungered, your heart was somewhere else. Somewhere far away, maybe in Texas.'

'Not Texas,' he said softly, 'but in the Arkansaw Valley...'

John Bartlett lit a stogie and pushed the box across to his ramrod. He said, 'Reckon it was the best news I had in years, when Black Sam came a-runnin' an' said yuh-all was ridin' in, Tracey.'

Rebel took a cigar and bit off the end and nodded soberly.

'We got through, John, but not without some trouble – some loss...'

'I saw when yuh-all rode into the yard, that Jimmy and Lovelace wasn't with the rest. Does that mean...?'

'It means they cashed in, John. This is part of the cost of drivin' a herd northwards.' Rebel straddled a hard chair and leaned his arms across the back. 'Jimmy gave his life helpin' us in a fight,' he said softly. 'But Lovelace – wal now. Mebbe it was my fault for takin' 'em to Santa Fé, for we found him in an alley with a knife in his ribs!'

'I figgered on losses, Tracey, both in men an' stock. That's why the whole business had to be on a strictly volunteer basis. Love-lace? Wal, I guess he might've wound up the same way down here. But Jimmy Yoakum – I'm dam' sorry, Tracey...'

'We also lost Rede Blackmer, but thank God not in the same way. Right now he's in Stage City an' married.'

'By Gregory! How come? But mebbe yuh better let me have the full story, an' I'll git Black Sam t' fix yuh somethin' to eat.'

Bartlett listened attentively to the details of their adventures, their hardships, their failures, and their success. Presently, when Tracey had finished the meal which Black Sam had brought in, he turned wearily to the rancher and laid the poke of gold on the table. 'Dam' near to twen'y thousand bucks there, John, thanks to Rosina an' Rede.'

'Yeah. An' thanks to the little Mex girl in Santa Fé!'

'Ah, John. Carlotta is a fine girl–'

'But the golden-haired witch as caused half the trouble – *she's* the one that's got yuh pinin'...?'

'I reckon.' Tracey moved over to the long windows, stood gazing out across the cattle-dotted range, and Bartlett said, 'How about *her* feelin's, boy; how do yuh know–?'

'I don't!' He whirled and thrust hands deep into his coat pocket. 'I only know what Rede said, when he came chasin' after us! Esther showed up in Stage City more daid

194

than alive. Said she was lookin' fer Long Rail, fer Tracey Rebel…'

'Goddamit, Tracey! *Yuh* ain't figgerin' to walk out on Long Rail – on me?'

Rebel said steadily, 'Rede was willin' to come back an' get his time from you, personal. Lovelace an' Jimmy didn't "walk out," an' so far, *I've* not suggested it.'

Bartlett sank down into the chair at his desk, gestured wearily with his big horny hands. 'Yuh gotta make some allowance fer me blowin' up like thet.'

'Mebbe after all, you got reason to, John.' He paced up and down the room, chewing the unlit stogie. 'Rede an' me was wonderin' whether you'd want another herd trailed north?'

'Sure.' Bartlett nodded his iron-grey head. 'Soon as the winter snow an' ice has gone, we'll have a right early round-up.'

'We was thinkin' of a fall trail-herd.'

The rancher said, 'That'd mean rounding up right away! The stuff's bin roamin' some since yuh-all bin gone. Take two-three weeks of hard ridin'–' Bartlett broke off suddenly and came to his feet. 'Look, Tracey, I kin jest about see yuh're honin' to ride that trail north clear to Stage City! But why load yuhself with another trail-herd that ain't ready anyway?'

'What you mean, John?'

'C'm on outside.' They stepped out onto

195

the veranda and the Long Rail owner pointed to Gila Creek a mile or so yonder. 'Yuh remember thet trapper's cabin we done found down there, Tracey? Why, with a bit of patchin' up, some furniture an' fittin's, I reckon it'd make a fine little home fer two!'

'What's goin' on in that head of yores, John?'

'Only jest thinkin' aloud, I guess…'

'Well, go on thinkin' aloud!'

'Figgered that a real good ramrod who's bin with an outfit all these years might like to live there – with his wife, of course. Come to think of it, boy, yuh ain't had overly much time off these last few years, hev yuh? What yuh say to two months with pay – free time…?'

Rebel grinned slowly. 'You mean time enough fer a man to travel fast to Stage City – an' back?'

'Sure! This girl, Esty. She ain't one as likes travellin' slow in a buggy, is she?'

Tracey's smile widened. 'Wait till you see her, John! She kin ride like a Sioux wind spirit an' fight like a mount'n lion.' He fingered his stubbled cheek reminiscently, and started to walk across the yard.

'Hey! Wh'are yuh goin', Tracey?'

Rebel turned and raised his eyebrows in mild surprise. 'Fust thing is to find the two bestest hosses,' he replied, and continued on towards the big corral…

It seemed strange, travelling this way again after such a brief respite. Rebel drew rein and rolled up a smoke and scrutinized the country from between down-drawn lids. It was not merely strange, he told himself, it was damnably dangerous, not to say plumb foolish.

All right. He had been lucky before, but on the trail drive he had fourteen tough Texans to side him. Now he was alone, and although a man could travel faster that way, he might yet ride as fast *into* trouble as away from it.

Nor was the Long Rail foreman entirely unhampered. For, besides the spare saddler, he led a pack horse on which Pinto and the rest had loaded grain, water, ammunition, food and blankets. They had not liked this business very much, and Tracey smiled as he recalled the uncurbed criticisms hurled at him by such old hands as Pinto and Mansella and Will Foruche. When men see their *amigo* ride out confidently and alone into danger, perhaps death, then their rough affection is measured by the anger they exhibit and their softly uttered oaths.

But a new anxiety came to squat on Rebel's shoulder, and as the miles dropped behind he pondered more deeply each day on the wisdom of this whole thing. Rede had not told him much beyond a few essential facts.

How could he have done? What was there to tell, save that Esther had ridden in, exhausted and hungry and desperate enough to have headed for the Red Light district? Only perhaps by the grace of God had the bearded and blasphemous Blackmer seen her in time and hauled her away from the sporting houses.

Maybe, Tracey reflected, Esther had made up a lie on the spur of the moment. God! Had she *intended*...? But no! He shook his head, convinced that was not the truth. There had been some kind of trouble in Corral Flats. Rede had said that. Esther had admitted as much. She had heard that Long Rail was in Stage City. Yet, when she reached there, after riding fifty miles in ten hours and with only the clothes she stood up in, it was to discover that the Texans had taken the trail for home. Only Blackmer had remained behind. Thank the Good Lord for Rede and Rosina, Tracey said over and over again as he rode northwards.

Each evening, before dusk descended, Rebel built a fire, quickly frying bacon and heating coffee. Long before full dark, he saw to it that no tell-tale flames or smouldering coals remained to pin-point his position.

On the eighth day he lay full length atop a scattering of rocks besieged by a small party of Apaches, out for coups and scalps. The skewbald pack horse had thrown up its head quite suddenly during the afternoon, giving vent to an uneasy nicker. Rebel had felt the sweat ooze from his body as his slitted eyes had sought and fastened on a bright red calico headband showing beyond a low wall of mesquite-stippled sandstone.

Almost unhurriedly he had veered slightly, and by sheer chance found the narrow path to the rock top. The bucks, mounted now, had charged from their place of ambush with blood-chilling cries, straight for the brash white man encumbered by his two extra horses, and desperately Rebel had urged them upwards, unleathering the carbeen as he rode. Almost to the top, the spare saddler tore loose from the lead rein, panicked by the wild yells and the bullets whistling so dangerously close. The animal wheeled and, for an agonizing moment, reared on the rim of a ledge before charging blindly into the on-racing band. It crashed head on into the first Indian pony and both went down in a cloud of dust and loose stone. Their squealing tore through the cacophony of discordant yells like a descant of death.

The buck had leaped clear, but Rebel, twisting in the saddle, had fired almost point-blank into the brown body, dropping it nearly at the feet of the on-charging braves. In the confusion he had succeeded in spurring on, upwards, hauling both horses and supplies to the temporary refuge of the basin- shaped rock summit. Here it had been possible to tie the horses to a piñon stump out of range and vision of the Indians below. At first these savages had been too eager for blood to allow the death of one of them to postpone the attack. With chilling whoops they had prepared to carry the fight to the white man, racing their mounts on towards the rocky pinnacle…

Now, Rebel schooled himself to take more careful aim. Maybe that earlier shot had been chancy, and a man couldn't count on two lucky shots in succession. He laid his sights on the war-painted shape just as pony and rider breasted the last short incline, no more than a score of yards away. He squeezed the trigger and quickly jacked a fresh shell into the firing chamber. Beyond the drifting gun-smoke the breech-clouted figure let go one piercing yell and pitched headlong, the steel-jacketed slug buried deep in his heart.

Rebel flicked the sweat from his eyes and slammed another shot, and this time dropped the wild cavorting pony in its tracks. It fell and lay still, forming, if not a barrier, then at least a delaying obstruction for those coming up behind. Again the Texan reloaded and fired, but the bullet screamed only perilously close to the nearest brave, and abruptly the Apache neck-reined his mount, calling hoarsely on his followers to retreat.

It was one thing to return to the village with a white man's scalp and his horses and supplies, or to boast of a coup. But this white man's medicine was very strong. He had a powerful and accurate 'shooting stick,' and already two of the warriors lay dead beside one of their fleet-footed ponies.

Tracey watched them draw away just beyond effective range. There were still eight of them left, and although he had reduced the odds he knew they were unlikely to quit so soon, especially in the knowledge that they had him cooped up with little chance of escape.

He reviewed the situation as calmly as possible, eyes watchful and probing, whilst he reloaded the carbeen and carefully laid the Colt's six-gun on a flat rock beside him.

Was this to be the end? he wondered, and then realized with a swift apprehension that only seven Indians were now visible some thousand yards distant.

He raised up from his prone position and made an even closer survey of the terrain. He glanced behind, down into the declivity where the two remaining horses were tied, and felt a prickling unease in the sudden quiet of the afternoon. The still air carried no sounds beyond the soft slobbering of the horses; the strike of their hooves on rock as restlessly they moved to and fro. It was then Rebel saw that one of the knots had slipped. A few more sharp, savage jerks of the roan's head and the horse would be free and likely plunging away from the scent of danger which now filled its nostrils. He turned and laid his sharp glance on the enemy. They were fanning out as though in readiness to start a fast circular action around this island of rocks. Not far away the spare saddler had limped to an uncertain halt, frightened and badly shaken after its collision with the Apache mustang.

Almost instinctively, Rebel placed his carbeen on the rock ledge and picked up the Colt's gun. He moved swiftly back to the horses and began working on the loosened rein. Both the skewbald and the roan smelt Indians sure enough. They nickered softly and side-stepped, and swung their rumps so that Tracey had to sheathe his gun and use both hands on the tie-rein.

He could not have heard anything, yet his head jerked up in the certain knowledge that death stood very close, watching. His narrowed gaze probed the mesquite-topped rocks as he half-knelt by the horses, and sweat rolled from every pore of his tensed body. The Apache crouched in a narrow fissure, a squat, fearsome figure. Murder and hate stirred the muddy depths of his jet eyes, and from his right hand a keen-bladed knife gleamed in the slanting rays of the sun.

In that infinitesimal moment of time between shock and swift reaction, Tracey knew that only by leaving his breech-loader behind had the buck been able to scale the well-nigh sheer rock-face over to the right. Then Rebel's hand dropped to the holstered gun. He had it clear of leather a second after the Apache leaped forward, knife upraised. On the instant of drawing, the Texan had straightened up. The Apache lunged forward for the death thrust, and Tracey, unable to line his gun, parried the blow and felt the tip slice the skin of his upper arm. He side-stepped swiftly as the Apache rolled like a cat on the earth and leaped back onto his feet. He was six yards from Rebel. There was no time for niceties, and Tracey fired the Navy Colt at point-blank range and saw the buck sink and slowly fold into a lifeless shape at his feet.

He wiped the running sweat from his face and saw to the loads in his gun, and stepped across to his look-out point. The scene had changed, even in so short a time, and Tracey Rebel's heart sank as he saw a fresh band of mounted bucks riding full tilt towards the seven who stood waiting beyond the talus slope at the rock-base.

Rebel licked his dry lips, even as his brain sought a way out. He stuffed the six-gun into its holster, picked up the carbeen, and ran back to the horses. Quickly he withdrew a leathern poke of ammunition and untied one of the canteens. It seemed a futile thing to do if he were about to die. That bunch down there were strong enough now to rush him from two directions. They would know well enough that he could not hope to deflect a two-pronged attack. Nor even would he have the power to resist a single spearhead charge along the upward winding path. True, he might get two or three of them, no more.

Resolutely, he hefted the Spencer carbeen. One brown-skinned rider below had deliberately or inadvertently drifted within range. Tracey dropped to one knee and took cold, careful aim and squeezed and fired. Grim-faced, he saw the Apache keel over and slide from the blanket-covered pinto. It was the signal for a concerted attack. They were sure enough going to make this lone white man pay for the four braves he had killed.

The leader of the newly arrived party rode a fleet-footed palamino. And at once he raised his voice above the surrounding babble, issuing harshly barked commands.

Rebel hugged the carbeen close to him. He thought, 'This is it, Tracey boy, after all! Oh, God! If I could've seen her jest once more! Why, if that helion Rede was here alongside me, we might–'

He wondered suddenly why they delayed.

And then came the reason. Over the hot, late afternoon air, a bugle blew its thin-sounding defiance, and Tracey fired a half-dozen shots in rapid succession and laughed aloud and let go his breath in a gusty sigh of relief.

Below, a buck was watching from a low rise, and twice he signalled back to the sub-chief before turning his pony around and rejoining the band. The Texan watched and wondered if the Indians might try to take him before the cavalry came up...

But the raw-boned Captain Phinney who commanded the scout detail from Fort Sumner had eleven years' frontier experience behind him. From his twenty-five men he had quickly sent four men and a trumpeter hurrying south-eastward along a dried-up creek. The remaining nineteen men, split into two small columns, had managed to approach within a mile or so of the ambuscade. Distantly, the trumpet sounded the call to charge, but for once the Apaches had been out-figured and out-manoeuvred on their own ground. Phinney came up over a low ridge to the north-west at the head of nine men, and the Indians were all set to give fight.

Over to the north-east Sergeant Brennan and ten troopers were stirring the dust above a narrow defile and racing in to close the trap. The Apaches started in firing at the two converging columns, and Rebel's lips compressed as he saw one blue-clad rider topple from his charging mount.

At a signal from Captain Phinney the men reined in to a grinding halt and slid from leather. The horseholders ran forward and the troopers spread out in line of skirmish.

Rebel fired again, though with small hope of effecting real damage, for the redmen had swung well clear of the rock cluster in an effort to dent the cavalry attack.

At this instant the line of troopers let out a rattling yell and fell into the charge, their Springfields blasting a way forward. The thunder of guns echoed around and over the mêlée, and Tracey saw the Apaches race their mounts in a desperate effort to break through. He saw brown bodies rise up on their blanket-covered mounts and fall. Others wheeled their cavorting ponies, firing and seeking to kill the yelling blue-clad troopers.

The big carbeens of the Army rolled up a heavy thunder. Apaches were scattering and beginning to flee. Rebel quickly untied his roan and went into the saddle in a flying leap and put the horse to the downward twisting path, and at the talus slope he hauled up and sent a withering fire into the backs of the now routed savages. Sergeant Brennan suddenly appeared twenty or thirty yards ahead of the Texan and fired twice, and Rebel, reloading, saw another tawny naked shape fall away.

For a while it had been a mixing of blues and browns, with the grey gun-smoke and the yellow dust rising and spreading over the bloody scene. And then, quite suddenly, it was finished, and a kind of silence crept back into this powder-drenched clearing seven-eight miles south of Fort Sumner.

Rebel saw redmen and horses and two or three bluecoats lying like shapeless daubs of paint on a gamboge canvas, and he was mildly surprised to hear the trumpet, near this time, blowing recall. Captain Phinney rode up, his face a mask of alkali dust and his teeth showing white in a smile which belied the snapping words. 'What the hell are you doing alone, in Injun country?' The troopers were coming back, caring for their casualties and mounting up. Phinney peered closer and snorted. 'By God! I might 've known. Aren't you the puncher who trailed those longhorns up from Texas and–'

'And camped for the night outside Fort Sumner!' Tracey grinned. 'Sure.'

Sergeant Brennan rode up alongside, saluted and made his terse report, and Phinney nodded.

Brennan looked at his superior and then at Rebel. 'The Texan we saw some weeks back, sir?'

'Yes.' He turned to Rebel. 'We didn't see

you return...?'

Tracey shook his head and wiped the sweat and dust from his face. 'We sold that herd at Stage City, Cap'n. Then we cut across to Santy Fé. After that we hit the trail fer the Nueces so almighty fast–'

'Yes.' Phinney spoke in the driest voice. 'If you're heading north again so soon, you had best ride back with us.'

'I'd shore be glad to, Cap'n.'

'This is Sergeant Brennan of D Troop. He will advise you what to do.'

12

NOT EVER AGAIN

Rebel could see the pencils of smoke, pale against the early evening sky; smoke from the stove-fires of Stage City. He remembered that just beyond these low, grassy folds, the town lay a bare mile further on.

As soon as Tracey rode in he saw that something was very much amiss. Way back along the trail he had heard something that might have been gun-shots. But they had sounded so far distant, no more than faint echoing pops, and he had shrugged away the thought of trouble in connection with Stage City.

Now he took in the scene before his eyes with a sharp understanding. Several ponies were racked a short way from The Golden Fleece; beyond these, Main Street was almost devoid of ponies or rigs. He glanced at the shattered plate glass; jagged splinters were all that remained of more than one store window. Roof awnings and uprights had been scorched and splintered in many places along the way, and suddenly he heard a crescendo of noise from beyond the batwings of The Golden Fleece. Two-three shots blasted out from somewhere, and the sound inside the saloon increased both in volume and tempo. Someone, Rebel thought, had figured on 'treeing' Stage City, and it looked like they were doing it thoroughly.

He spurred the roan forward and urged the limping pack horse alongside, and slid from leather and hit the ground like a cat. The uproar now was near to deafening at such close quarters, and from down-street more shots sounded and a man's high-pitched yell rose and then stopped abruptly. Tracey's hand touched the gun at his hip as he pushed through the batwing doors into a scene of savage destruction. Men were fighting each other with every and any weapon that came quickly to hand. He saw the Town Marshal, Broge Slattery, cut down by the wicked slashing blow of a gun-barrel wielded by a figure strangely familiar.

In a corner of the room several of Rosina McCall's girls huddled together, white-faced. A black-garbed, evil-looking man held them there at the point of a gun whilst the battle raged around. For a moment Rebel found it difficult to distinguish friend from foe, and then he saw Rede Blackmer rise up out of the mass of litter and inert bodies, blood streaming from his nose and mouth. He swung his huge fists and caught two men between them, and then Rebel saw

210

something that turned his eyes a dull red. Rosina was at the foot of the stairs, her ink-black hair loose, her eyes dark smudges against the pale olive of her skin. She had raised a big, single-action Frontier Colt, and a huge bearded fellow swept it from her grasp with one blow of his paw-like hand. He showed yellow teeth in a wide, loose grin and caught Rosina by the shoulder. She swung away, her face burning with a fearful anger as the flimsy dress ripped from her shoulders.

It was impossible to use a gun without endangering lives indiscriminately, and Rebel tore through the milling throng like a bull-steer on the rampage. He felt glancing blows, but for the most part his weight and strength and the fury in him carried him through to the stairs where the dark girl stood rigid against the balustrade, staring into her traducer's eyes with loathing and mounting terror.

Rebel reached forward and gripped the man's buckskin shirt with such tremendous force that the fellow was swung around and pulled in close against Tracey. And as their gazes met, sudden recognition flared in each man's eyes. This, Rebel knew now, was one of Charlie Dodge's men, one he had seen in that swift moment when he and Pinto had snatched up Esther from the outlaw gang.

There was no time to speculate on whether

Dodge was here in town with all his followers. Even now the split-second pause had given the outlaw time to throw up a guard to his bearded face. But nothing in human shape could have stopped Tracey Rebel right then. The Texan swung his fist in, low and deep into the man's solar plexus, and heard the rasp of his wind driven out through the gaping sagging mouth. He fought to suck in air but Rebel drove in again and again and stood the big man against the wall and went on hitting with a cold, calculated ferocity.

The outlaw was almost insensible, and Rebel stood back and crashed bloody knuckles into the whiskered jaw. He stood away, breathing deeply, and watched the limp mass slide into a heap on the floor.

He turned quickly, catching Rosina by the arm. 'Where's Esther?' he croaked, and the girl took a hold on herself and her eyes went to Rede who was still bloody but unbowed. 'Thank God – you're here, Tracey! Esther went across – across the street to Dunbar's, just – just before Dodge an' his killers...'

He nodded. 'Go on upstairs, Rose, an'–'

'No! No! Rede's here! I must–'

A man's voice rose above the din. *'Thar's thet bustard as stole the girl, Sid...'*

Rebel whirled, too late to avoid the bottle that glanced along his head and exploded in a shower of jagged glass and founting liquor. He lurched against the stairs as another man struck at him. He went down half-stunned, and seized the man's legs and brought the desperado on top of him, and crawled on him and got his hands to the man's throat and squeezed until the roughneck quit fighting, his face tinged a dark, reddish-black. A man's spurred boot lashed out at Rebel's head and the Texan rolled and got a tight hold and twisted until the man screamed and went down with a crash into the mass of struggling bodies and smashed furniture.

Somehow Tracey got to his feet and felt Rosina's steadying hand. He said thickly, 'How many men's Dodge got in town?'

She looked at him out of smouldering eyes and again sent her burning glance across to Blackmer's huge, lunging body. 'Somewhere around twen'y men, I guess, Tracey. Rode in two-three hours ago. But it's Esther I'm worried for. Go to her, Tracey! Dodge may've found her! We can manage...'

'How many town men you got in here, Rose?'

'Enough, Tracey, enough!'

They had to shout at each other to make their voices heard over the din. Rebel's searching eyes found the black-garbed outlaw who had been holding a gun on the frightened saloon girls. Just for a moment the way was clear; no brawling, swaying figures stood between the Texan and Dodge's henchmen, and Tracey drew the Colt's gun and fired across the noise and dust-laden atmosphere. He saw the man clutch himself and slowly fold, the gun slipping unheeded to the floor. In the tumult Tracey's shot had gone by unheard, save by one or two men slugging it out close by.

'Get yoreself and the girls upstairs *pronto*, Rose. None of you's safe.'

'But–'

'Goddammit! Don't argue! I know these coyotes!' He swung away to the doors, and the way was blocked by a rugged sandy-haired man with eyes like dark pebbles.

'I remember you,' the man said. 'You jumped us on the Santy Fé Trail – jest fer a woman!'

'Move aside, mister,' said Rebel in a thick voice. 'I'm goin' out.'

'Try it,' the fellow said and smiled coldly. He swept a rock-like fist at the Texan's face and Tracey rolled his head and took a glancing blow that made his ear sing. He brought up a hard knee to the man's crotch and heard him groan and saw him fall back, the bronzed face turning a pasty yellow.

Rebel drew his gun then and slammed the long barrel against the outlaw's head. A chair swished through the air and splintered to matchwood against the wall a foot away from the Texan; then he was outside on the boardwalk and the street was no longer deserted as before.

He saw men shape up to him out of the gathering dusk, and from The Golden Fleece came a warning shout. 'Hey, Whitey! Hey, Lance! Look out for this Texan. He took Charlie's girl!'

Rebel sidestepped and spun round and threw a snapshot over the saloon's batwings. He had to take the risk if he was to get Charlie Dodge. He swung back as boots pounded close by. Two men launched themselves towards him. He ducked away and slammed the barrel of his gun in a wide, savage sweep and saw through a haze of fury that the foresight had opened a deep channel in the first man's face. He fell across the boardwalk steps and lay there sobbing and cursing, and again Rebel ducked away just in time. He threw up the gun and called, 'Watch out – back up!' But the other man had already sprung forward and Tracey's gun slashed out again and descended on the man's head with a sharp cracking sound.

Men backed away in the face of the Texan's fury, while a few of the townmen called out to Rebel, remembering his name and anxious to identify themselves.

Across the way the lamps had been lit in the Lewis House and Dunbar's Emporium and Tracey went across the street at a dead run and hauled up as though he had hit a wall.

From the Emporium Charlie Dodge had

emerged, his left arm tightly encircling Esther Masterton's waist. She was fighting like a savage, and then Dodge hit her on the point of the jaw and she sagged limply between his arm and body.

'Dodge!' called Rebel.

Dodge let go his hold and the half-senseless girl sprawled across the walk. Dodge started walking towards the Texan. He remembered all right, and he came on, steadily staring at Tracey through the fading daylight. In the middle of the Main he slowed and moved his head fractionally as though, after all, he was not here to fight. But he took one quick and sudden step to the side and clapped his palms against the tied-down holsters with force enough to create a strong echo on the air. Rebel saw his legs sag at the knees, his elbows crook. Somewhere, far away, he heard Esther's voice calling. But he heard nothing else and he saw no one but Charlie Dodge twenty yards away, and he brought the Navy Colt up in the fastest, smoothest action and triggered his shot. Then he heard the double roar of Dodge's guns and lead whistled the wind against his face and Dodge teetered and keeled over like a drunk unable to maintain his balance. One of Broge Slattery's deputies came pounding down the street, a shot-gun held ready, and from outside The Golden Fleece Blackmer's voice boomed, 'Hey! Tracey! We got 'em fixed–' His words were drowned in the sudden sharp rataplan of hooves. Men turned quickly and saw the shadowy shapes of horses and riders as the remnants of Dodge's badly mauled gang hit the dust.

Rebel wiped the sweat and powder smoke from his face and re-holstered the gun and grinned at Blackmer and turned towards Dunbar's. He saw her half-raised up from the dust, and the light streaming from the shattered windows behind made a golden nimbus of her hair in the violet dusk. Men's voices found strength and rose to a crescendo around him, and then a shot rang out and poured its white heat from the gun of the dying Charlie Dodge. Rebel felt the lead slam into his chest and pain seared his whole body, and the strength ran out of him and he fell into Main's churned-up dust.

It seemed as though he were on a tree-top swaying in the breeze, and the sun was bright in his face and he remembered that other time in Santa Fé – the tapers and the oil lamp and Carlotta. He opened his eyes and saw the decorated ceiling, and somehow, even before he turned his head, knew that he was back in The Golden Fleece.

There was a good deal of talk going on around him, and his blurred gaze lowered and he was looking at Rede and Rosina and Broge Slattery who wore a clean white

217

bandage around his head.

'Esther?' Rebel said and looked at Rosina's smiling face and knew the fullness of a profound relief.

Doc Atter shoved forward, bent low over the bed, holding Rebel's wrist, watching his face. 'Only got the bullet out a few minutes, Mr Rebel. You shore got to take it easy and rest...'

Rebel closed his eyes and again he was swinging, but more gently this time. A deep pain lay inside his breast and burned and then receded, and he felt only a softness and warmth and her perfume came to him and filled his nostrils. It could only be that he was delirious, yet he opened his eyes again. He had to make sure.

She was standing there by the bed, gazing down at him with shining eyes, and her hair was a shimmering mist of gold around her shadowed face. He turned his head and saw only the empty room beyond, and vaguely wondered at the passage of time.

'Esther,' he said, 'I...'

'Don't talk,' she whispered, and knelt beside the bed, and suddenly her arms were about him and her breasts against his head so that he felt the quick rhythm of her heartbeats.

Presently she drew away and he looked at her and saw that her eyes were wet with tears.

'Why,' Tracey said, 'what's wrong, Esty? What have I done to you?' He looked away and added softly, 'I figured I was right in comin' back, Esther, but only fust off. Nearer I got to Stage City the surer I was that I'd lost...'

'You ask me what you've done to me?' Her voice was as low and musical as a soft, rustling breeze. 'Nothing, Tracey, 'cept broken my heart and – and mended it again.'

'You don't figger me still as...'

'Oh, my darling!' She laid her soft warm lips on his bruised face and lightly touched the dark hair that curled a little around his temples. 'Was any woman ever such a fool?' she asked. 'Has any woman ever bin so blind?' She stirred and gently drew away, and Rebel said huskily, 'Don't leave me, Esty.'

He felt the heat of her lips on his mouth then, and in that kiss lay everything. And painfully his hand groped out and touched her hands, and though the tears she smiled and her voice was low-pitched and tender: 'I'll not ever leave you, Tracey,' she whispered. 'Not ever again for as long as we live...'

This Large Print Book, for people
who cannot read normal print,
is published under the auspices of

THE ULVERSCROFT FOUNDATION

BC	3/13
KE	2/14
KT	1/20